MW01109939

PRICELESS

Contributions by Marina Fontana-Hentz

PRICELESS

Sixty-Six Simple Stories of Reflection, Love, and Legacy

CARLOS FONTANA

TATE PUBLISHING
AND ENTERPRISES, LLC

This book is designed to provide accurate and authoritative information with regard to the subject matter covered. This information is given with the understanding that neither the author nor Tate Publishing, LLC is engaged in rendering legal, professional advice. Since the details of your situation are fact dependent, you should additionally seek the services of a competent professional.

The opinions expressed by the author are not necessarily those of Tate Publishing, LLC.

Published by Tate Publishing & Enterprises, LLC
127 E. Trade Center Terrace | Mustang, Oklahoma 73064 USA
1.888.361.9473 | www.tatepublishing.com

Tate Publishing is committed to excellence in the publishing industry. The company reflects the philosophy established by the founders, based on Psalm 68:11,
"The Lord gave the word and great was the company of those who published it."

Published in the United States of America

ISBN: 978-1-61346-494-6
1. Self-Help / Personal Growth / General   2. Body, Mind & Spirit / General
11.09.09

To the memory of my sister, Eurita Maria,
and my brother, Gilberto Paulo Fontana

Book Given To: _____

From: _____

Date: _____

Location: _____

Thoughts: _____

Acknowledgments

Many thanks go to my mother and father, for they always believed and encouraged me to go to faraway lands to learn, to grow, and to seek wisdom. They showed me the importance of faith and that vision is seeing first with the mind then the heart. They started my long formal and life education journeys by teaching me work and discipline at the family farm. Without any formal education, they became wise. Thanks to my two special daughters, Marina and Andrea, who have always supported and inspired me. It has been a great joy working with you on this project, Marina. Thanks to Adam Hentz for your help with the photos.

Special thanks to Cristina DaRos for being there when I needed someone to talk to. You have contributed a lot more than you will ever know.

Special thanks go to my partner Don Mercer. Our different personalities and experiences have been extremely complementary and effective in our undertakings. It was a pleasure and honor working with you on your book *Follow to Lead*.

Very special thanks go to all the story contributors who took time to reflect on my question and share their stories for the benefit of all who will read them. The ripple effect of your goodness will last until the end of time.

To all the readers who will take the time to read the stories and reflect upon them. The world will be better when you share the simple things that impacted you deeply. Your giving spirits will outlive you.

The highest thanks go to God for never giving up on me during all the struggles and trials in my life. You always guided me and helped me to find a way even when there seemed to be no way. I can now see You daily. You led me to a life of simplicity, silence, and solitude. This book is the proof that a true dream does come true!

Contents

Foreword

Anyone who has ever met my dad has learned two things about him very quickly. First, he is a man of many words; to say he likes to talk would be an understatement! Second, he is a man of many questions; no matter how much he likes to talk, he likes to listen even more! This is why I was not surprised at all when he first told me his idea about writing this book. One of the many lessons he has taught me during my life is how important it is to be able to carry on a conversation with someone. Not only is it important to know how to initiate or speak with someone, but it is even more important to know how to listen to someone. We can learn many life lessons simply by closing our mouths and opening our ears, and many times, these lessons come from the unlikeliest of people.

In the increasingly fast-paced world we live in today, the art of listening has very much been lost. Society has ingrained in us the idea that it's all about oneself and to get where we want to go, we must trample on everyone else. This has caused us to become so self-absorbed that we rarely take the time to listen; instead, we are consumed with doing all the talking. Instead of asking what we can do for someone, we ask: what can they do for me?

This book contains stories and lessons from many different people from vastly diverse backgrounds. My dad spent countless hours asking people a very simple question, and in return he received answers that we can all benefit from hearing. Some of the people whose stories are in this book come from those who he has known for a very long time, but others were just chance encounters with people who were in the right place at the right time. Each and every story contained in this book is worthy of your attention and reflection. The stories come from ordinary people like you or me, but their lessons are extraordinary.

I am very grateful that I had the chance to collaborate with my dad on this book. I have learned so many important lessons from the stories, and I have tried to take those lessons and apply them to my own life. If you learn nothing else from this book, I hope you take away from it the importance of understanding how even the smallest of actions can have the greatest of effects, extending out to others like ripples in the water. Try your best to apply the lessons contained in this book, and your life will be forever changed. You will find that in the end it's not the money spent that was important but the meaning behind the action that was done. So get out there, find someone who needs your help, and do something. You will probably find that you are the one who learns the greatest lesson!

—Marina Fontana-Hentz

Introduction

WHY ANOTHER BOOK?

If you are anything like me, you still have several books around you that you have not read yet. Most books are not read past the introduction. On the other hand, many books are read. Books can and do change lives. According to a 2007 CBS News story, citing a government report, Americans are reading a lot less. Reading skills were on the decline across almost all education levels. What is disturbing is that on the average, Americans ages 15 to 24 spend almost two hours a day watching TV, and only seven minutes of their daily leisure time on reading. Why do so few of us read? One of the reasons is our lack of hunger to learn and to do more. Imagine buying books for about ten dollars with nuggets of wisdom teaching us how to find meaning in our lives. When we buy a book like *Man's Search for Meaning* by Dr. Viktor Frankl, we are in fact buying eighty-plus years of a great man's experience for the price of a meal.

WHY THIS BOOK?

The short stories were obtained from the hearts and minds of people just like you. The stories will make us think more, reflect more, love more, and do more things that will continue long after we are all gone into eternity.

A great life is the sum of the little moments that occupy our memory banks forever. At some point in our lives, we all start to think about living lives of significance and not just making a living. Many people have gone out and made fortunes. Making a difference is a lot harder than making money! People in these short stories made a difference, and I bet you have too if you take a few minutes to reflect on your life.

Most stories are about love, generosity, and giving. Big givers will always leave great memories behind them. It is true that the more we give, the more we get in life. In one form or another, sooner or later, what we send out into the world comes back to us multiplied either for the positive or the negative we do unto others. When it is all said and done and the potato salad's gone after our funeral, we will be remembered more by what we gave and the legacy we left behind than by the size of our bank accounts. Go ahead and start paying forward if you want to get paid backward.

During the past two years, I have been blessed with the time and health to go out and take thousands of pictures of nature and meet and talk with over one thousand individuals from all walks of life. My brain was fed with the incredible beauty that God created within nature and humanity. In the digital age we all live in now, anyone can become an amateur photographer. People crave for someone to ask about them and to hear their story. Why don't you go out and try? You will never be the same person again. We have so many communication tools at our disposal, and yet people are more lonesome today than ever. There is so much human and natural beauty all around us. It is so humbling to compare the marvelous things man created versus the magnificence of God's creations. Is it time to redefine what quality of life really is?

This book is all about reflection, love, and leaving the places we go better than we found them, touching the lives of those we encounter on our journeys. The people that really made a huge difference in this world, the giants we all read about and for whose shoulders we stand on, were people just like us. When asked what they would do differently if they were to live their lives again, they responded that they would reflect more, they would love more, and they would do more things that would continue after they were gone. We are all here for a purpose. Find yours, and go on a journey to create your life story. The day you can say, "This is what I am going to do for the rest of my life," is the first day you have really lived.

There is a lot of worry and fear in the world today. Employees fear losing their jobs. People are worried about their health, the state of their personal finances, and the relationship with their loved ones and their friends and associates. The time has come to be a lifelong learner. Get on a system of learning. Find a university of life for life. We live in a global community now. Borders no longer exist. Problems and issues are common and so are many solutions. Many people are stressed out and have poor health. Stress is reduced by everyday learning and growing. We all would love to have more security. Security is no longer where it used to be. Security today is in the quality of our thinking and the speed of our learning and sharing with others! My 2010 New Year's resolution was to meet two new people and give out a book every day. I kept my promise, and what a difference it made in my life. Everyone has something to teach us. Everyone has a story to tell. Encourage them to tell their story and really listen!

WHAT WAS THE BEST VALUE YOU GOT IN YOUR LIFE FOR ABOUT TEN DOLLARS?

The question led to people thinking, reflecting, and telling a short story. The ten dollars represents a small sum of money that we spend frequently and often without much thinking about it. So little thinking is done in the microwave society we all live in. We are all bombarded and overloaded with information. Ninety percent of the information out there is of little or no value. It just occupies the precious space in our brains. The key is to get information that leads us to proper thinking. The right information changes our thinking and leads to knowledge. Applied knowledge is what leads us to wisdom. Wisdom comes from reflection, experiences, and learning and living proven principles from those that have come before us and those around us. Success and significance in life is predictable; unfortunately, so is mediocrity.

HOW CAN YOU GET THE MOST OUT OF THIS BOOK?

Take the time to read one story a day or read them all at once. You choose! Reflect on each one. Answer the question after each story. Ask your own questions. The book is yours; write all over it. It is yours now to leave your marks on its pages. Imagine one hundred years from now when your great-grandchildren find this book and read your notes on the edges of the pages.

HOW WERE THE STORIES COLLECTED AND SELECTED?

The sixty-six priceless short stories were obtained by asking the following simple question during sit-down sessions, phone interviews, and mail message exchanges: What was the best value you got in your life for about ten dollars? Many answers were similar. The most common answers were a book, a marriage license, a meal shared with someone special, and money given away to a stranger. Two-thirds of the people interviewed did not have an answer. Out of the one third that did have an answer, most had the answer right away while others had to think for a few minutes. A few had stories they would rather not share and were grateful for being asked the question. For some, the first answer was not their final answer. Some said they would send it later. I did receive a few answers after sending reminders. Some may still be thinking about it!

The stories included in this book cover important areas in our lives like faith, family, friendship, fun, finance, freedom, and following.

The stories were organized into three themes: reflection, love, and legacy.

The stories will help you to become a more creative giver.

Before you dive into the short stories, answer the question yourself: What was the best value I got in my life for about ten dollars?

Now, go ahead and enjoy the sixty-six simple stories!

STORIES OF REFLECTION

Jesus on the Cross

The best money I ever spent was for a cross with Jesus on it. I look at the cross daily and realize Christ died on the cross for our sins. Those who believe in Him can have eternal life. How many people are willing to die for others? Well, Christ did so He could free us from our sins, and now billions of people around the world can have eternal life. People in the armed forces risk their lives every day, and many die for our freedom. I find it incredible when someone is willing to die to save others. Many people in New York City did exactly that during the events of September 11, 2001. This is why I am working for Christ now. I call myself one of God's detectives by talking with people and sharing with them little reminders of what Christ has done for us!

Joy comes from serving others.
When have you risked your life for others?

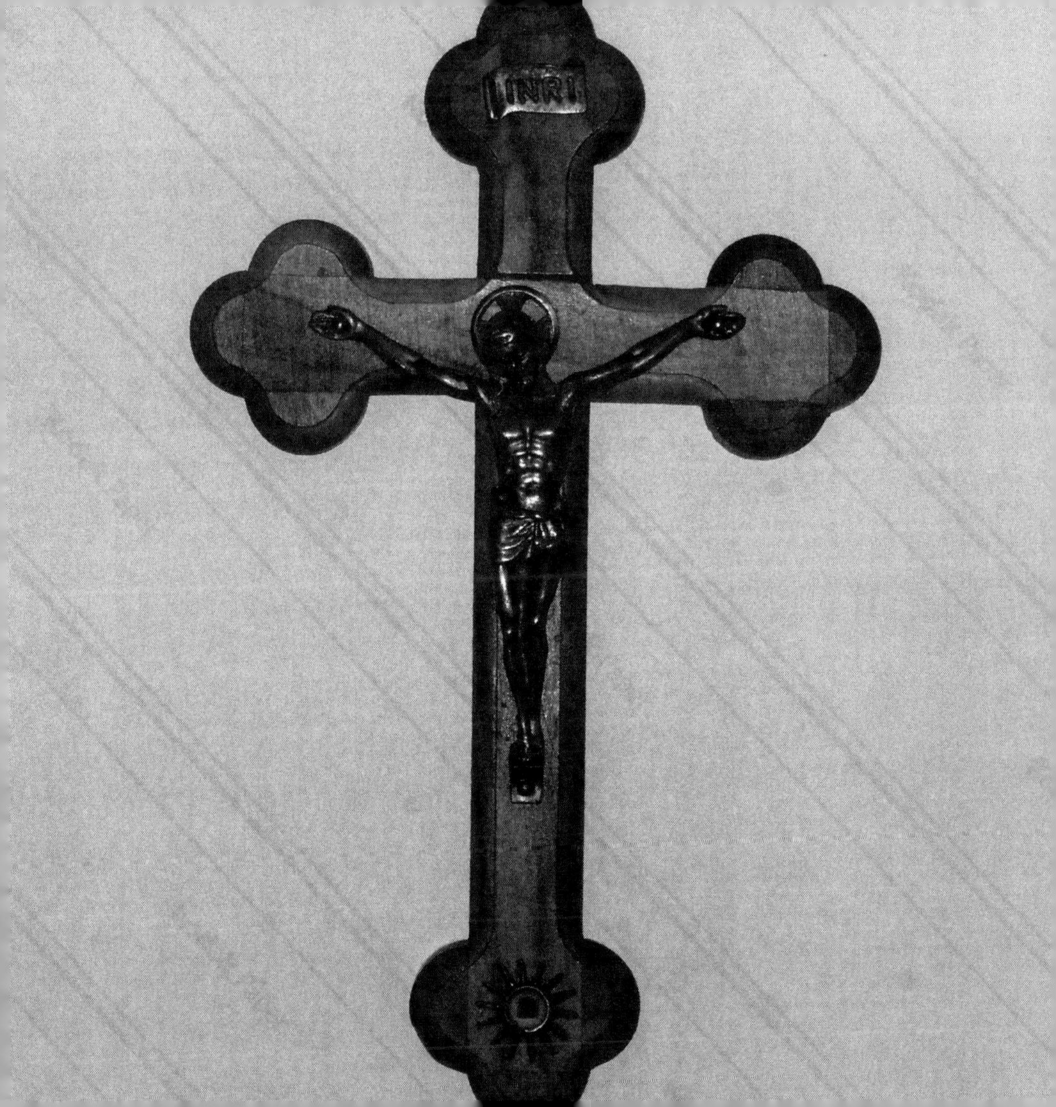
INRI

A Prayer Book

For me, the best value for ten dollars was a prayer book I bought many years ago. Prayer is the source of faith. Prayer gives us inspiration and courage. Prayer gives us hope, and, most importantly, prayer gives us belief in and love for people. Prayer helps us to reflect and to connect to a higher power. That little prayer book helped me to become who I am today!

**Prayers have motivation and inspiration power.
What is your favorite and most powerful prayer?**

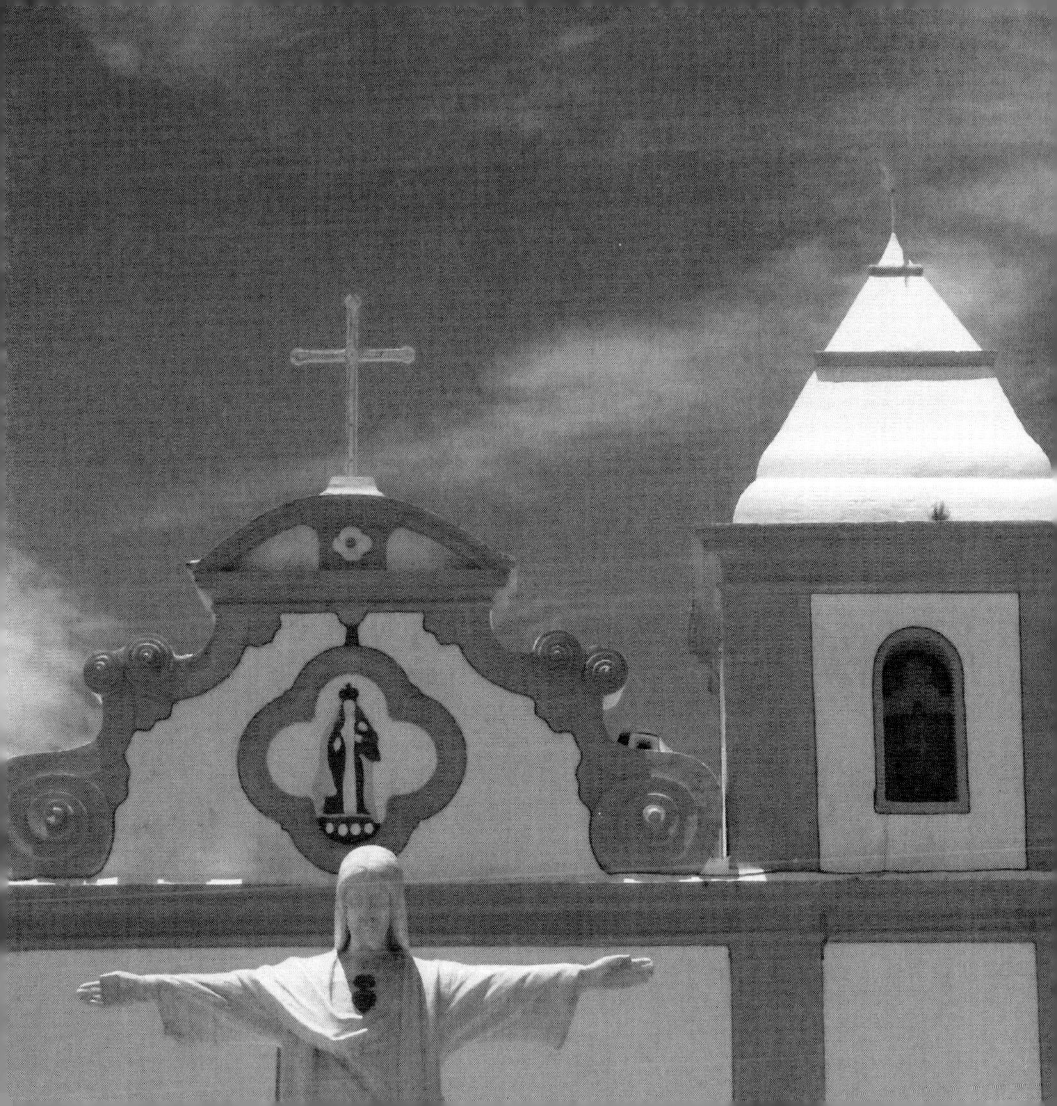

Clothing for Disabled People

When you do social work like I do, you work with people that have very little. The agency I work for does not have the extra money for us to buy things for the people we care for. The best money I ever spent was to purchase clothes for the disabled people that I take care of. I purchase clothing in garage sales and give them as gifts to the mentally and physically disabled. I know the people I work with really well, so I give them what they really need, not just what they want. I can see their joy when they get something they need after they accomplish small tasks. It is very important to reward them for their work and their small victories. You can see they feel happy with the rewards for the work they do.

We stretch, grow, and prosper by giving.
What have you learned from working or
interacting with people who are disabled?

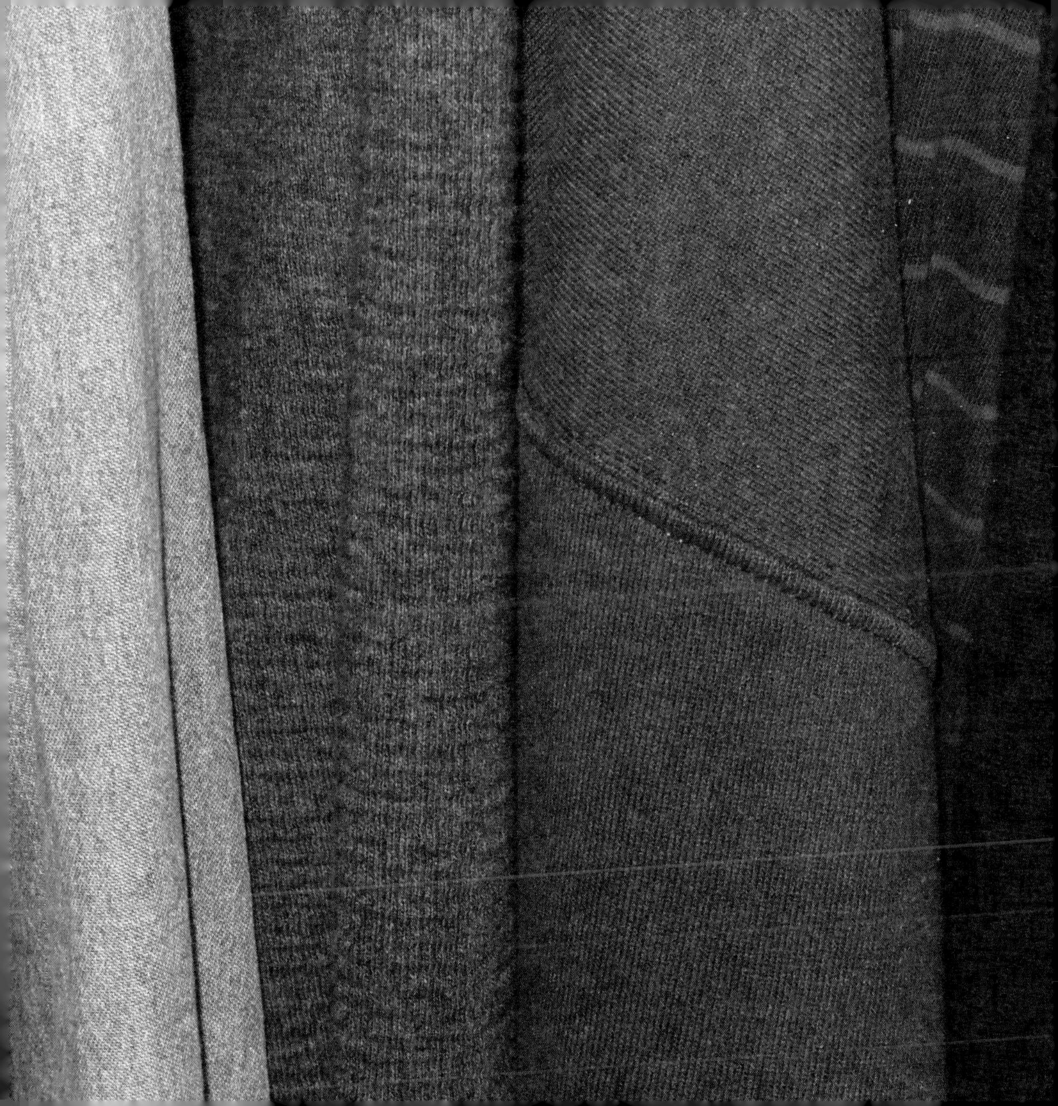

A Leadership Meeting with My Dad

Best value for ten bucks? I know, about six years ago my dad and I attended a leadership meeting. I saw my dad so excited and happy because he had renewed hope in his life. He said he could now see a victory coming in his life. What was so special about that particular event? Well, that was the last time I spent with my dad before his accidental death shortly after. I will never forget the last day I spent with my dad. That special time had a profound effect on me. Now I am working hard to help create victories for our family and for those around us. Once people see hope and belief in us, they can go and do the same for others around them! It is like magic!

**Sharing quality time leads to lasting memories.
What are your best memories from the
experiences with your parents?**

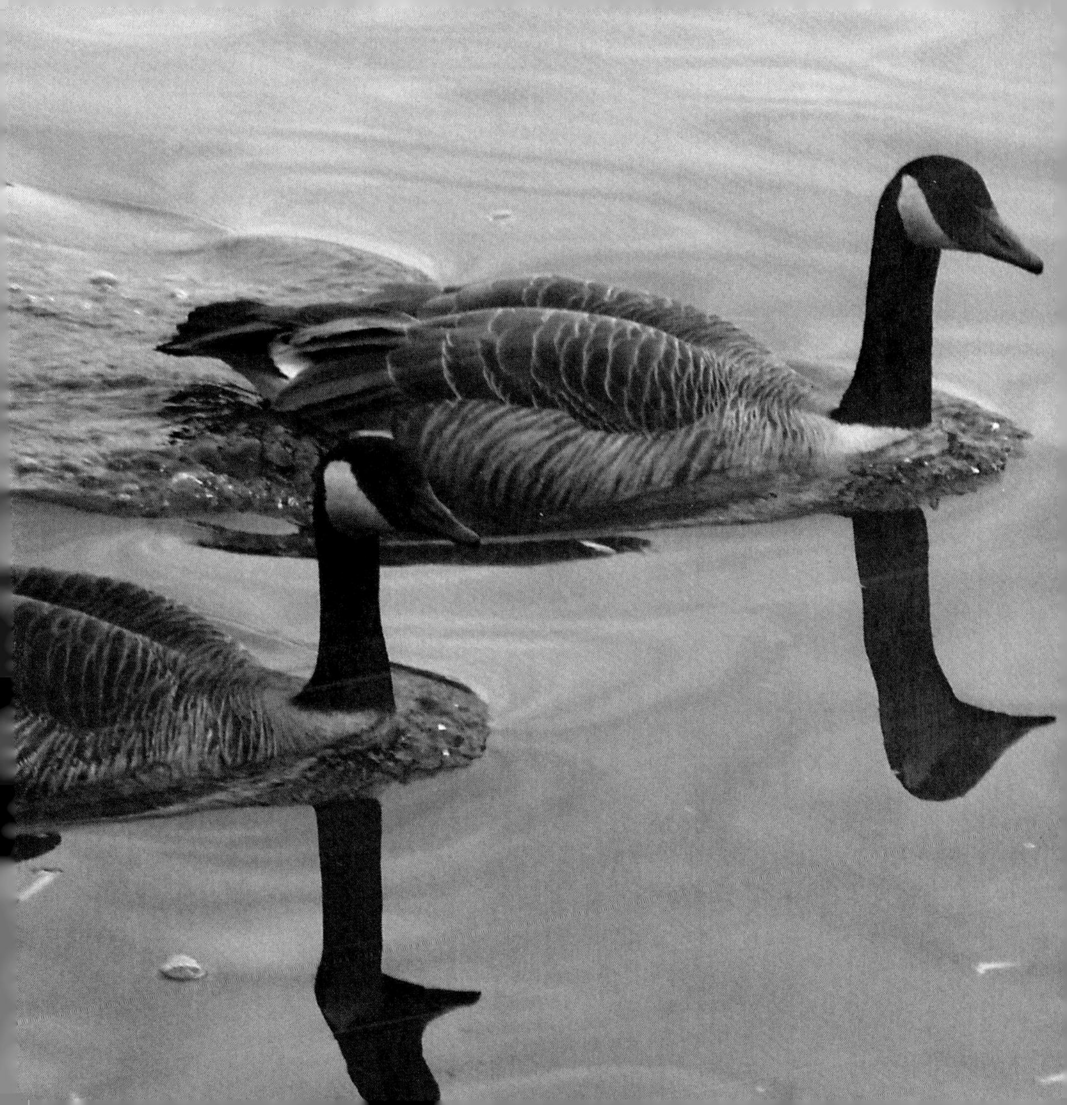

A Loan from My Dad

In 1949, my dad loaned me ten dollars to help me with the down payment for my first car. Upon payment, I was surprised that my dad had charged me interest. Right then and there I learned a life lesson about debt and interest. The lesson I learned was how important it is to avoid debt or pay off debt as soon as possible. Since I learned that lesson, I have passed it on to my nieces and nephews and others around me!

**Mistakes are repeated until lessons are learned.
What is the importance of living a debt-free life?**

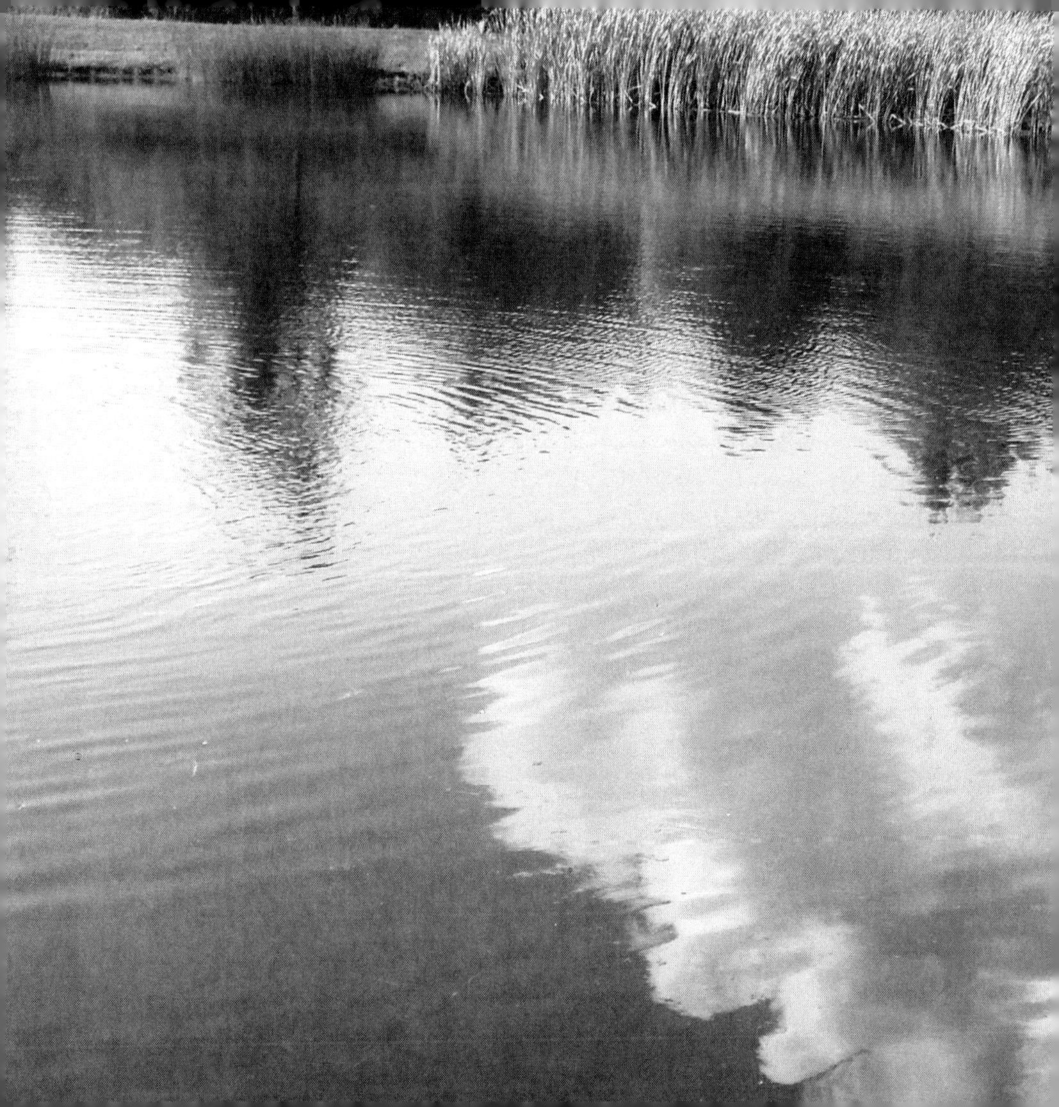

A Train Ticket to Visit My Grandmother

The best ten dollars I have ever spent was to buy a train ticket to visit my grandmother. During the visit, I asked her some deep questions about our family, our heritage, and our culture. That visit motivated me to start writing out my family tree. My grandmother has a great memory, and she told me many stories about my family, and I learned that I have Cherokee Indian blood in me. That visit also helped me to become spiritual and a more peaceful man. I attribute my sense of peace to a growing hunger for spirituality and other important aspects of my life.

**Knowing where we come from helps
us to determine where we are going.
What have you learned about your family heritage and culture?**

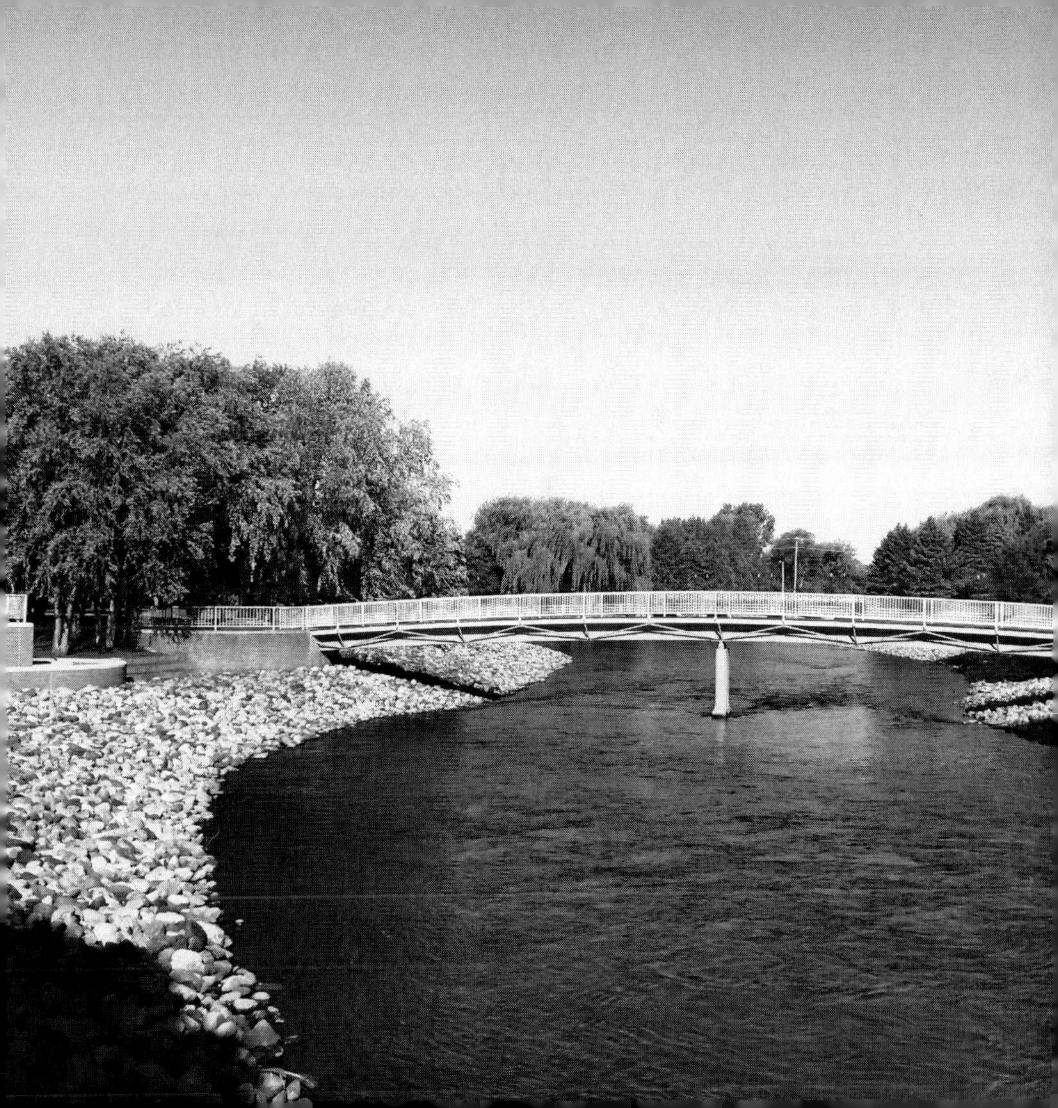

Pizza for Hourly Workers

Years ago when I was working with hourly workers at a food manufacturing plant, I realized I needed a way to show appreciation and respect for project work people had done for me. I decided that I would buy pizza for everyone. My positive intent counted, and I learned that the material value was not as important as the thoughts behind the action. I gained loyalty and trust over and over from the hourly workers. A shared meal is a powerful way to connect with people. There is a sense of community in us when we eat the same food.

**Eating occasions are opportunities to create strong bonds.
How can you develop trust and loyalty
from those important to you?**

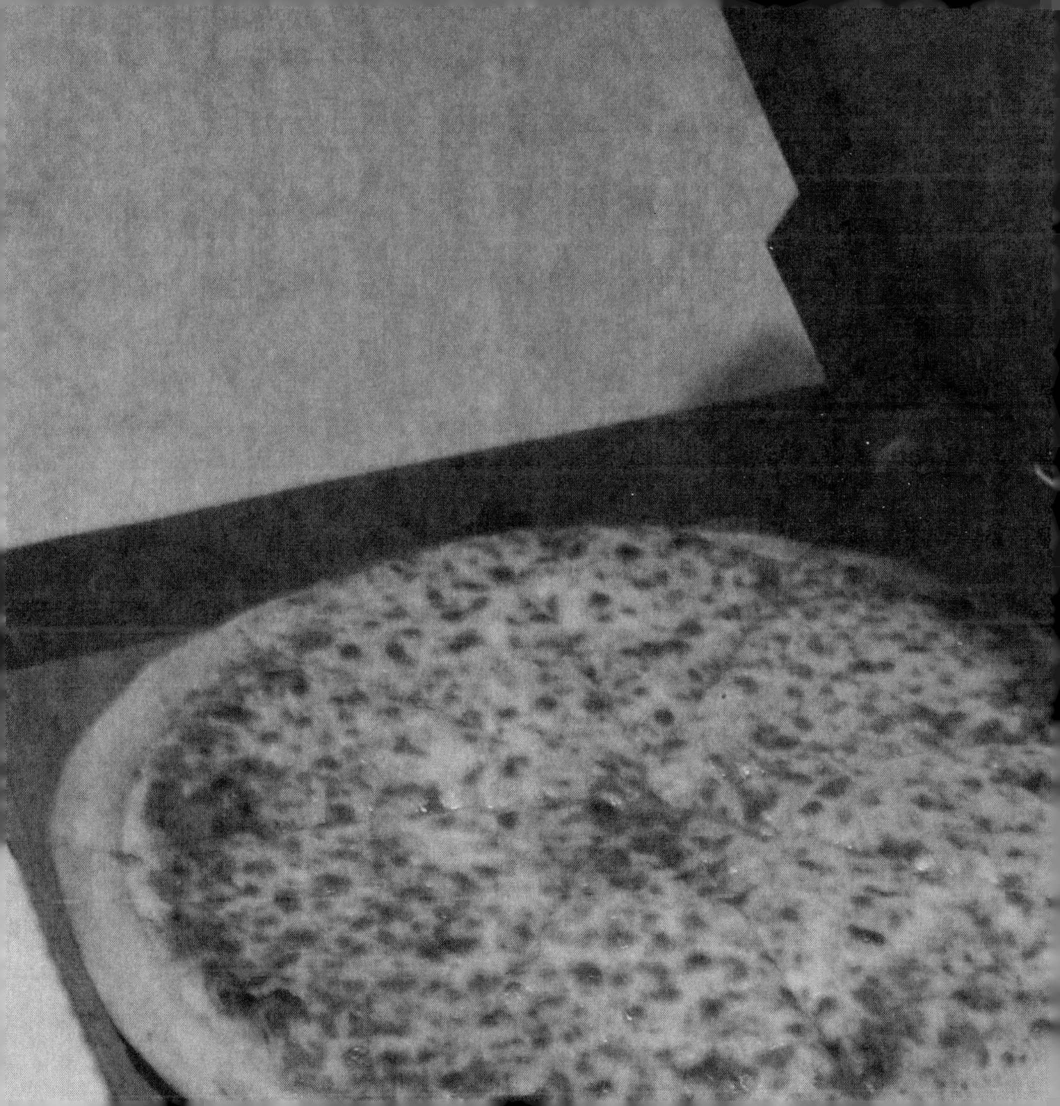

An Effects Pedal for My Guitar

I bought an effects pedal for my guitar when I was fourteen years old. The pedal allowed me to really enter into the realm of rock guitar. I got into a band shortly thereafter. Guitar playing has brought so much joy into my life that is beyond measure. I really get a kick out of it when folks come up to me at gigs and tell me how much they enjoy seeing me play now.

Special effects can be very effective.
What are the little things in your life that
have impacted you the most?

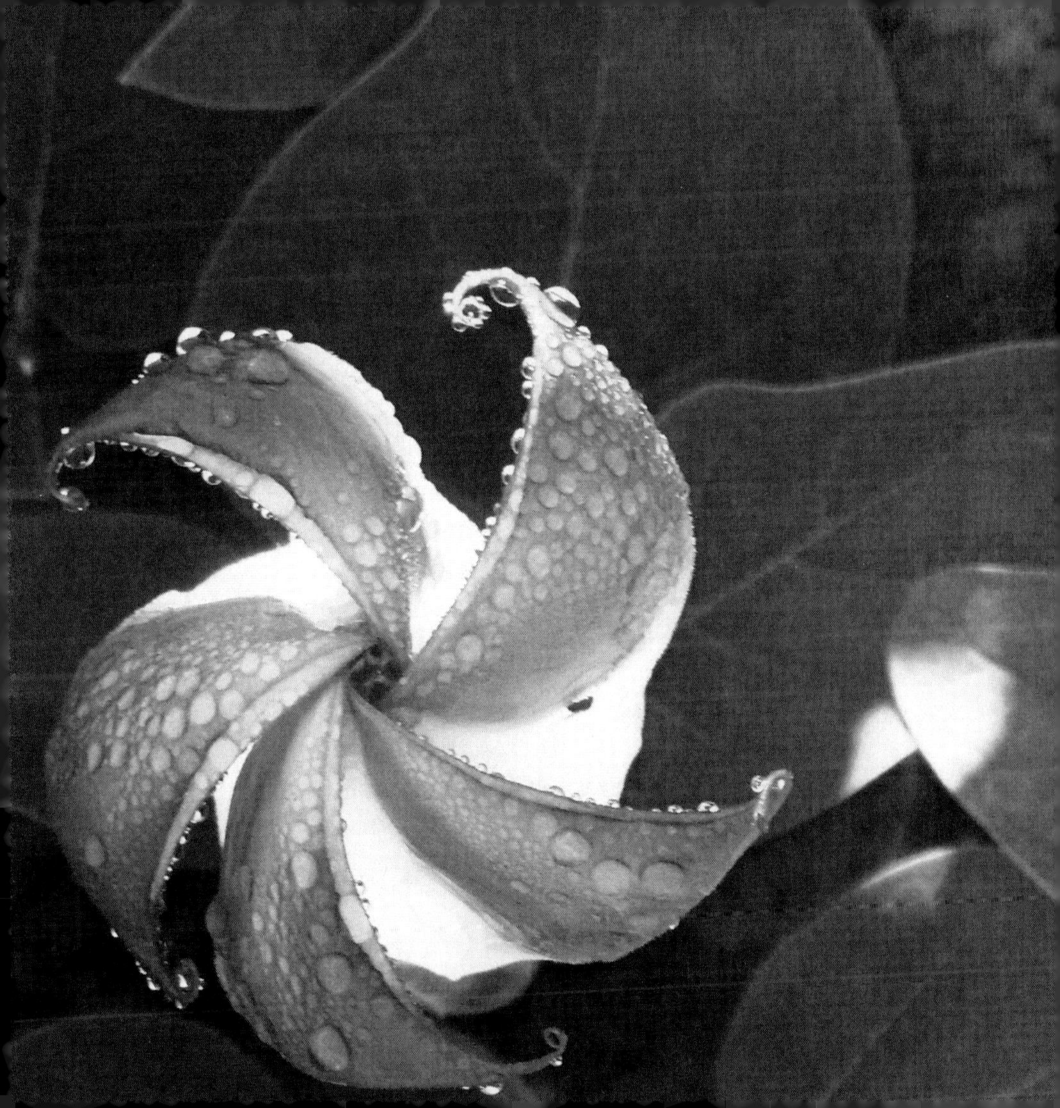

Movie Tickets

Last December my husband and I went to Traverse City to celebrate our one-year wedding anniversary. I had the idea of going to see the movie *It's a Wonderful Life* with James Stewart. It was the first time my husband had seen the movie. It was great to have someone I loved with me at the end of the movie when I cried. I used to watch this movie with my dad. He still calls me every year when the movie is on TV. We loved the experience of watching it together. The movie reminded me of the wonderful memories I had with my dad. Also, it reminded me not to wait until we lose important things in life in order to value them. My parents divorced when I was young, and my mother had cancer. I took great advice from this movie since life is too short not to be fully lived! We will now watch this movie every year. We need to be reminded that the memories that we create are what really matter in our lives.

Special celebrations lift up our spirits.
What movie brings back the best memories of your loved ones?

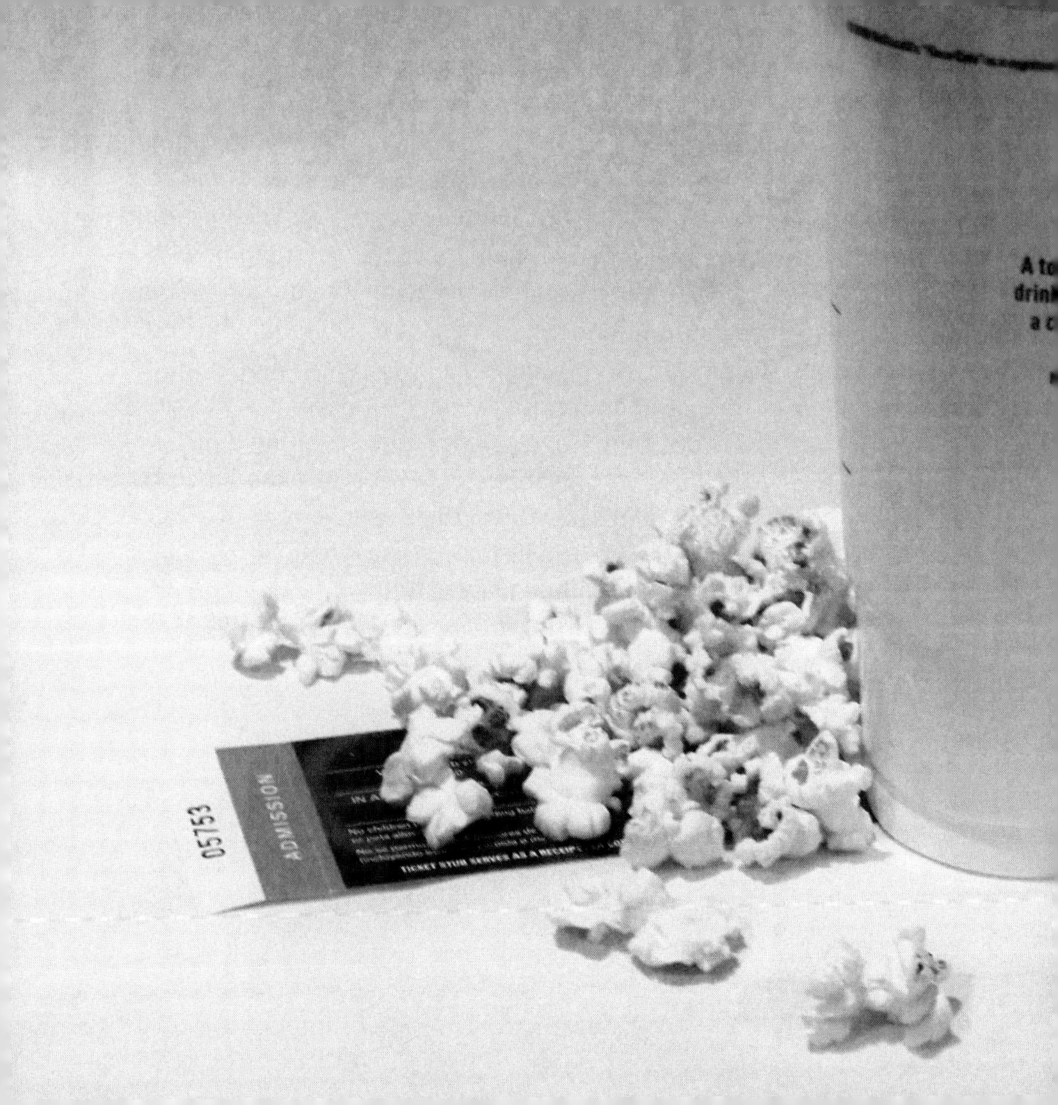
05753
ADMISSION

A Self-Improvement Book

The best $10 investment that I ever made was the book *Think and Grow Rich* by Napoleon Hill. I became aware that "thinking" was the key to success and that using the mind and learning how the mind works were very important. Don't dwell on your problems; instead, devote your mind to solutions. I'm not sure if "thinking" was even considered before I read this book. We can buy someone's life experiences and wisdom for only a few dollars. Besides, we do not have thousands of years to live acquiring our own experience. We can have one thousand years of experience by learning from others, especially from their mistakes!

Books can change lives forever.
How often do you share your top book titles with others?

DEVELOPING THE GLOBAL ORGANIZATION

THE LEXUS AND THE OLIVE TREE · UNDERSTANDING GLOBALIZATION

ROBERT JOHNSON

INNER WORK

LEADERSHIP JAZZ · MAX DE

REAL LEADERSHIP: THE 101 COLLECTION · JOHN MAXWELL

MAXWELL DORNAN

BECOMING A PERSON OF INFLUENCE

LEADERSHIP GOLD

JOHN MAXWELL

JONES

A Bus Ticket

I had always wanted to go visit the city of Curitiba in Brazil. I had heard many people talking about this city for years. I used to read in newspapers and magazines about this beautiful ecological city, and I wanted to get to know the city, but I lived over six hundred miles away. Later on in my life, I relocated to the beach town of Camboriu to pursue my master's degree program there. This now meant that I was only two hours away from Curitiba, so one day I decided to drive and spend the day there. Upon arrival, I got on a city bus, which took me on a twenty-five-mile city tour, taking me to the main tourist locations. I got off the bus several times and walked around and then got back into another similar bus. The bus ticket cost was about $10, but my experience was priceless. I repeated the trip to Curitiba many times to get to know new sections of this great city. Now I am waiting to get on a cruise ship to work and continue my new discoveries. The truth is that the experiences in Curitiba had a lot to do with my choice of a career in tourism!

We can never have enough of nature.
How did you decide what profession to pursue in your life?

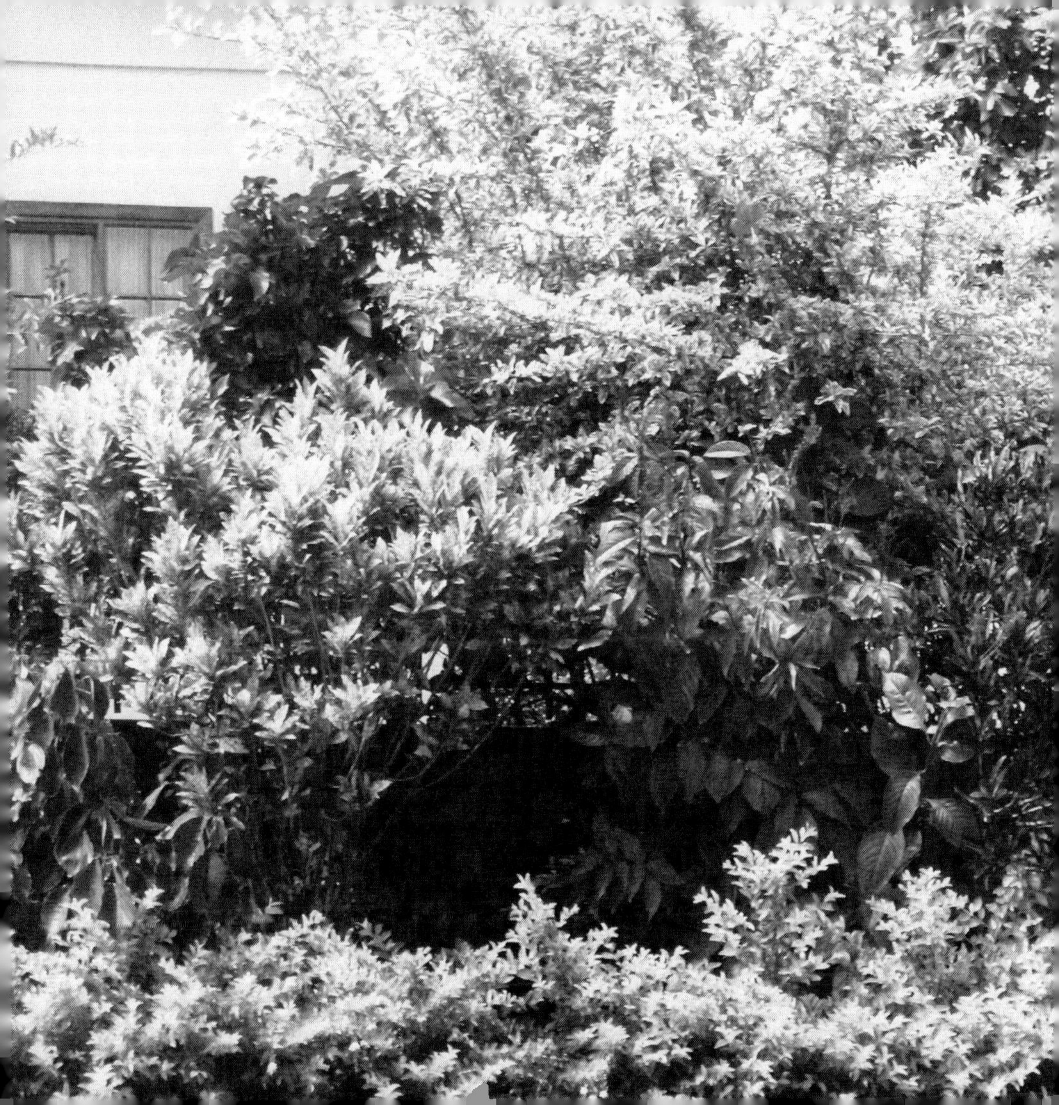

An Art Work Donation

I can tell you that I have done a lot of bad things in my past, and because of that I have spent more years of my life inside than outside of prisons. The longest prison term I served was for nineteen years when I was convicted for the second time of second-degree murder. I have done all kinds of drugs, but now I am drug-free. I have done a lot of wrong to others in my life, and I have hurt a lot of people. While I was in prison, I learned how to do different kinds of artwork. The art I do most is burning on wood and painting on clay. I started doing art in anticipation of needing money once out of prison. I found out that it was very hard to sell what I had made, so I started giving my art work to those who could not afford to buy it. My favorite subject to portray in art is humming birds, which I paint on clay. Helping others has helped me feel better about myself and also helped me to change who I am. I realized that God had forgiven me, but I have not forgiven those who I have hurt and I have not forgiven myself either. I am glad we are having this conversation because I realize now that I need to forgive myself and everyone else in my past. It is heavy baggage that I am carrying, and I realize I need to let it go!

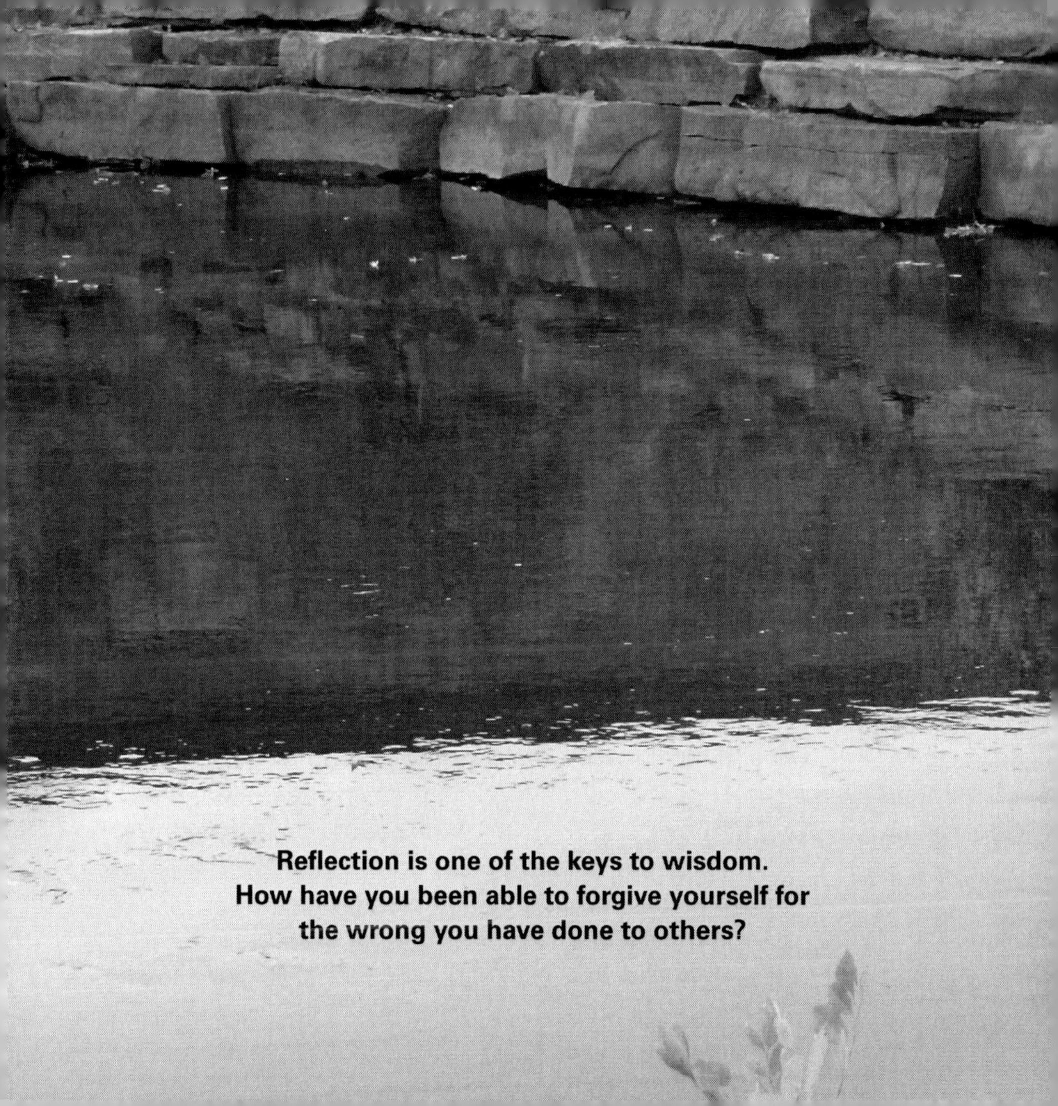

Reflection is one of the keys to wisdom.
How have you been able to forgive yourself for
the wrong you have done to others?

Money for a Poor Child in India

At this time in my life, I was working in Bombay. I knew Bombay very well because I had spent a lot of time there. I knew that India was known for having extremely poor people and beggars; very often they were children who were maimed by gangs and mafias who coerced small children to the streets. It is a business of the worst kind. Children are burned with boiling oil, blinded with charcoal, and have their limbs cut off. It is unbelievable! My local manager reminded me not to give money to them because they are known to succumb to fighting among them to steal the money the weaker ones receive. One of these kids, who had only stumps for legs, followed me for over an hour, looking at me with piercing eyes. I gave in, and without anyone seeing, at least I thought, I gave him $10. I regretted it instantly because half a dozen other kids jumped on this poor little kid, stole the money, and left him crying. I tried to intervene, but the driver and my manager pulled me away. Other beggars were beginning to circle the car, and we were in danger. Those were the ten most expensive dollars that I gave to the poor child, and for me. I think about him so often!

The giver can sometimes hurt the receiver.
Did you ever want to help someone and
ended up hurting them instead?

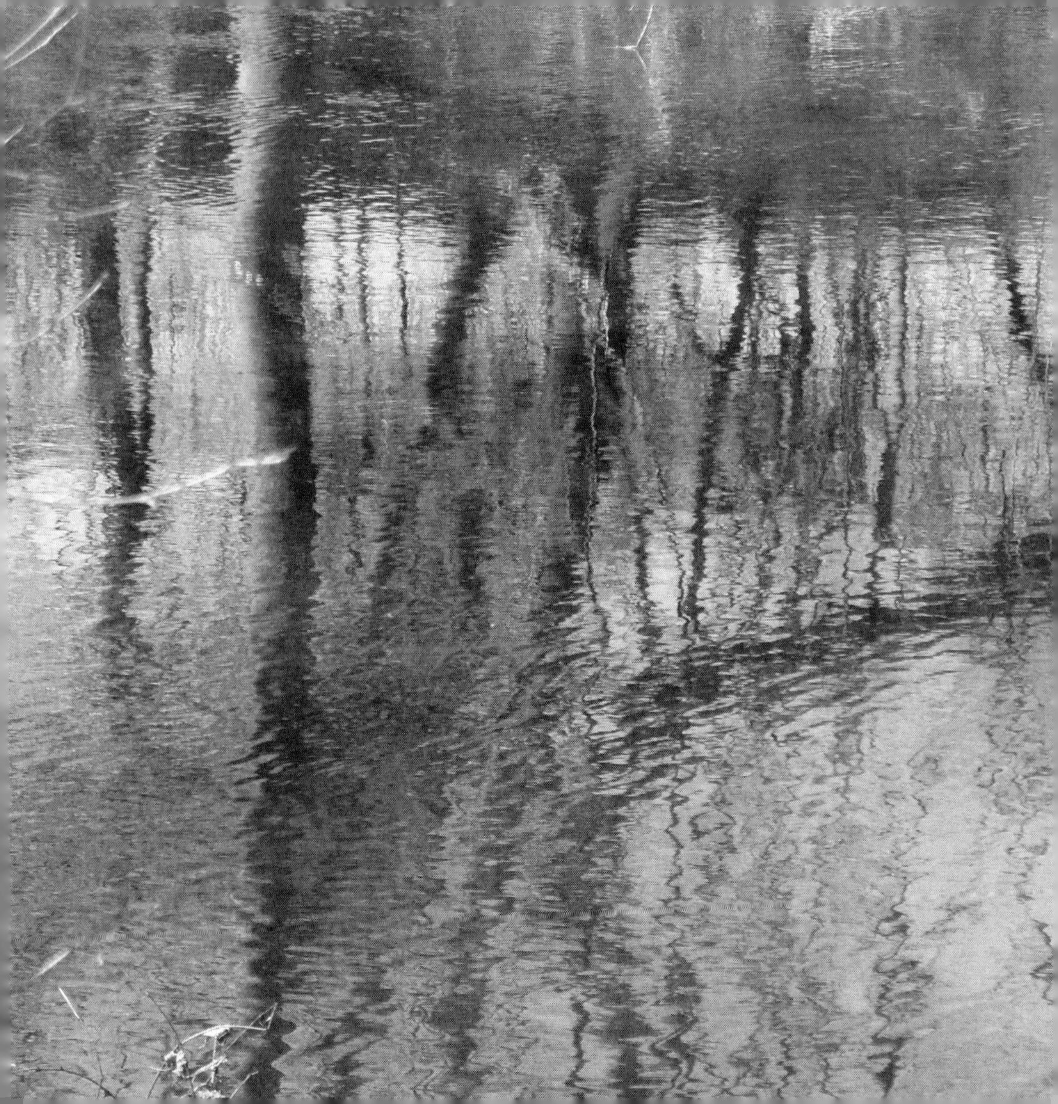

A Black-and-White TV

I had just arrived in the USA and was going to start my doctorate degree and did not know English very well. The black-and-white TV I bought in a garage sale ended up being my free English professor. The TV spoke for hours without charge. I did not understand everything, but I was getting used to the language. When the time came to test my English for foreigners, I passed the test and did not need to take English classes before starting my doctorate program. I was able to take less credit hours, which saved money and gained me time! Not a bad investment!

TV can be used for learning a new language.
What is the most helpful gadget in your life?

A Special Mug

A few years ago I was walking by a coffee shop in Mexico City and decided to go inside. Some things that caught my eye were a few coffee mugs. As I looked at the mugs, the one that I thought I had to buy had the following saying on it: "Life isn't about finding yourself. Life is about creating yourself." That big truth really hit me. It was like a bolt of lightning had struck me. Right then I had this urge to buy the mug because at that moment I found out I needed to act. I checked my wallet and realized I did not have enough money. The mug cost just a little over $10, so I ran to the office where there was an ATM machine to draw the money out. As I went back to the store, all I could think was that I hoped someone else did not stop in to buy the mug that I wanted. Now I drink my daily coffee from my special mug, read the saying, and think about what it is like for me and for many others that are trying to find themselves. I learned to take personal responsibility for my life, to stop wondering, and to start building my life. I realized that I need to be better every day. It is a daily reminder of my responsibility. I also realize that it is human for us to build our own lives. Because of a special mug, I found meaning in my life!

Build a life on a solid foundation.
What famous quotation has impacted your life the most?

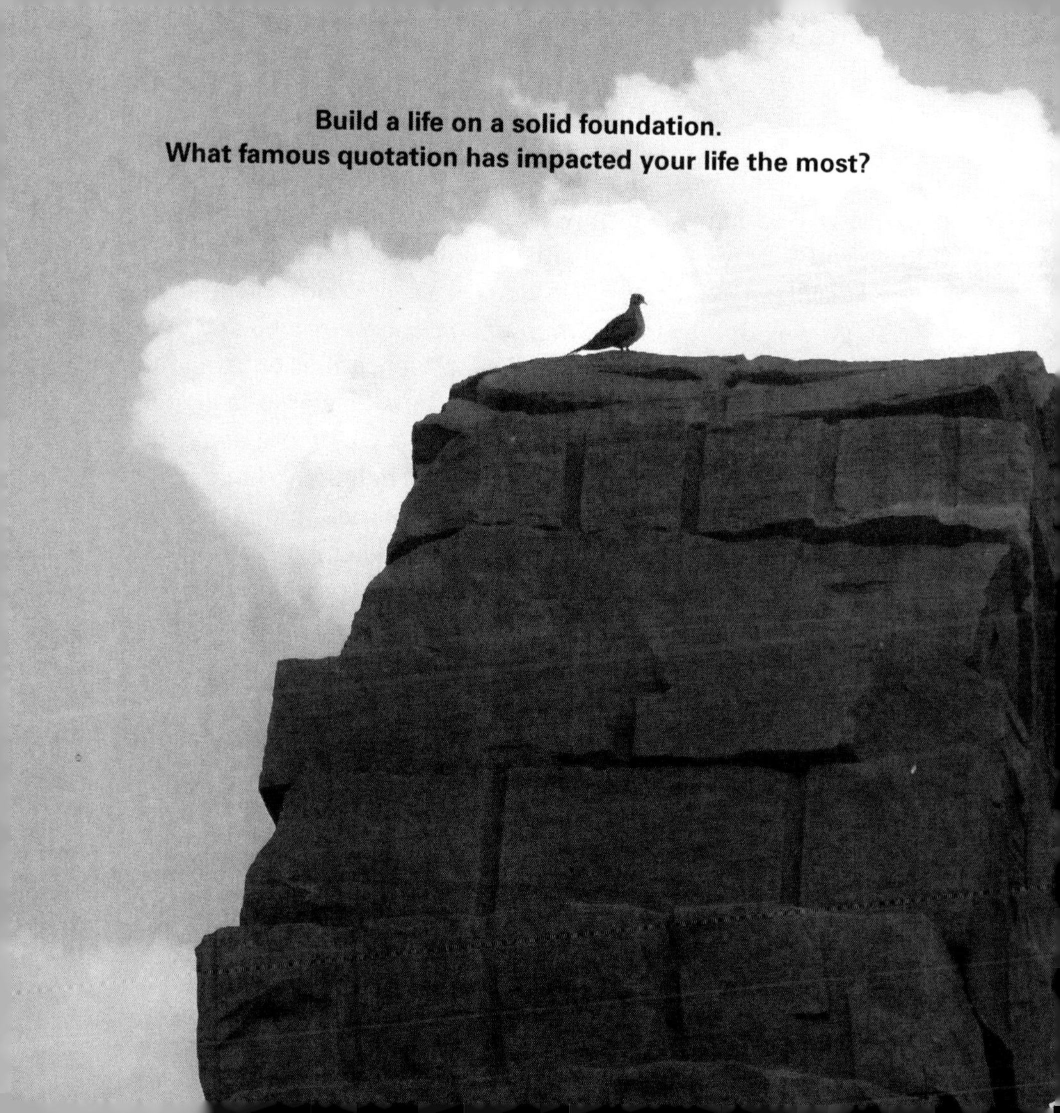

An Influential Book

In 1973, when I was fourteen years old, I used to save most of my weekly earnings, which was around twenty-five cents. At that time, and after my father's death, my interest in chess began. One day, I decided to "invest" my savings in a chess book. The first one I bought was *Bobby, the Triumph of an Obsession*, a book written by Luciano Camara, in Spanish. The influence that book had on me was enormous and, in fact, would mark the start of a lifelong passion and love for the game. I started to play more and more seriously, studied in a disciplined way, and definitely changed the way I saw things. I read the book several times throughout the years, and now, more than thirty-five years later, I can surely say that the passion that such a book created in me, helped me a lot, not only in achieving relevant goals in chess like becoming the first grand master in postal chess in the area of Mexico, Central America, and the Caribbean and reaching twice the Latin American championship, but also in my professional and personal life. I am so grateful for the passion that started that day, and I hope it will continue until God calls me home.

The simple is not always obvious or easy.
Which book do you identify most with?

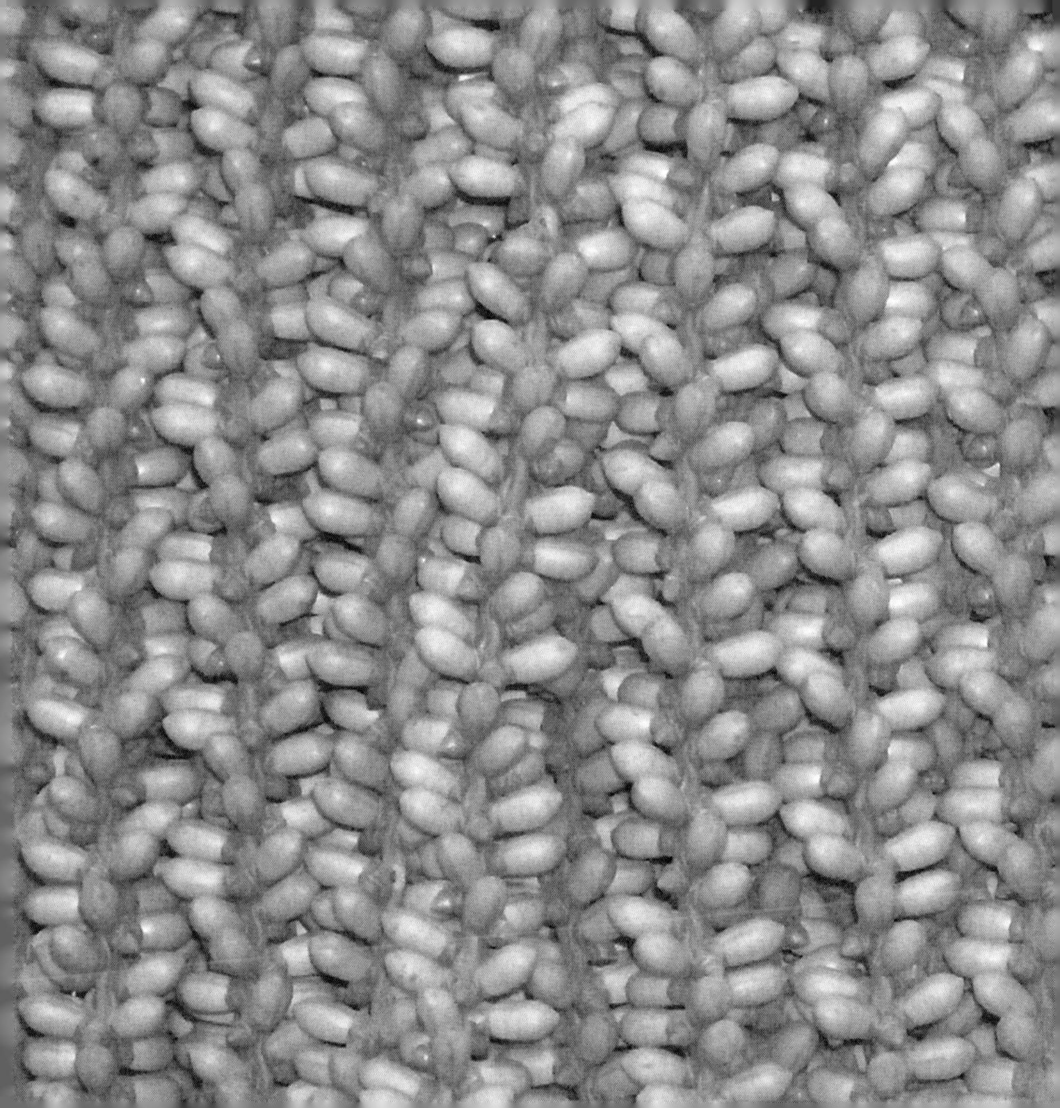

Gas for a Field Trip

I took a day off from work to go to school with my younger daughter on a field trip. Once there, I ran into my older daughter's schoolteacher, who I had not seen for one year. The teacher asked me to sit down and talk with her. We had an extremely nice visit. We had no agenda. She gave me such a peaceful feeling during our pleasant conversation. She was so calm and so full of grace with an unusual sense of peace. I told my husband about our conversation when I got home. The following week the teacher was in a car accident and died. The special conversation we had often comes to my mind, and it is a reminder to take time with people and to slow down. The teacher gave me the gift to slow down at a time I was extremely busy working as a buyer in my corporate job. I now feel the responsibility to let others know about the importance of the gift of time and passing it on to others.

Friends in conversations are like flowers on a sunny day. How often do you slow down and give quality time to a friend?

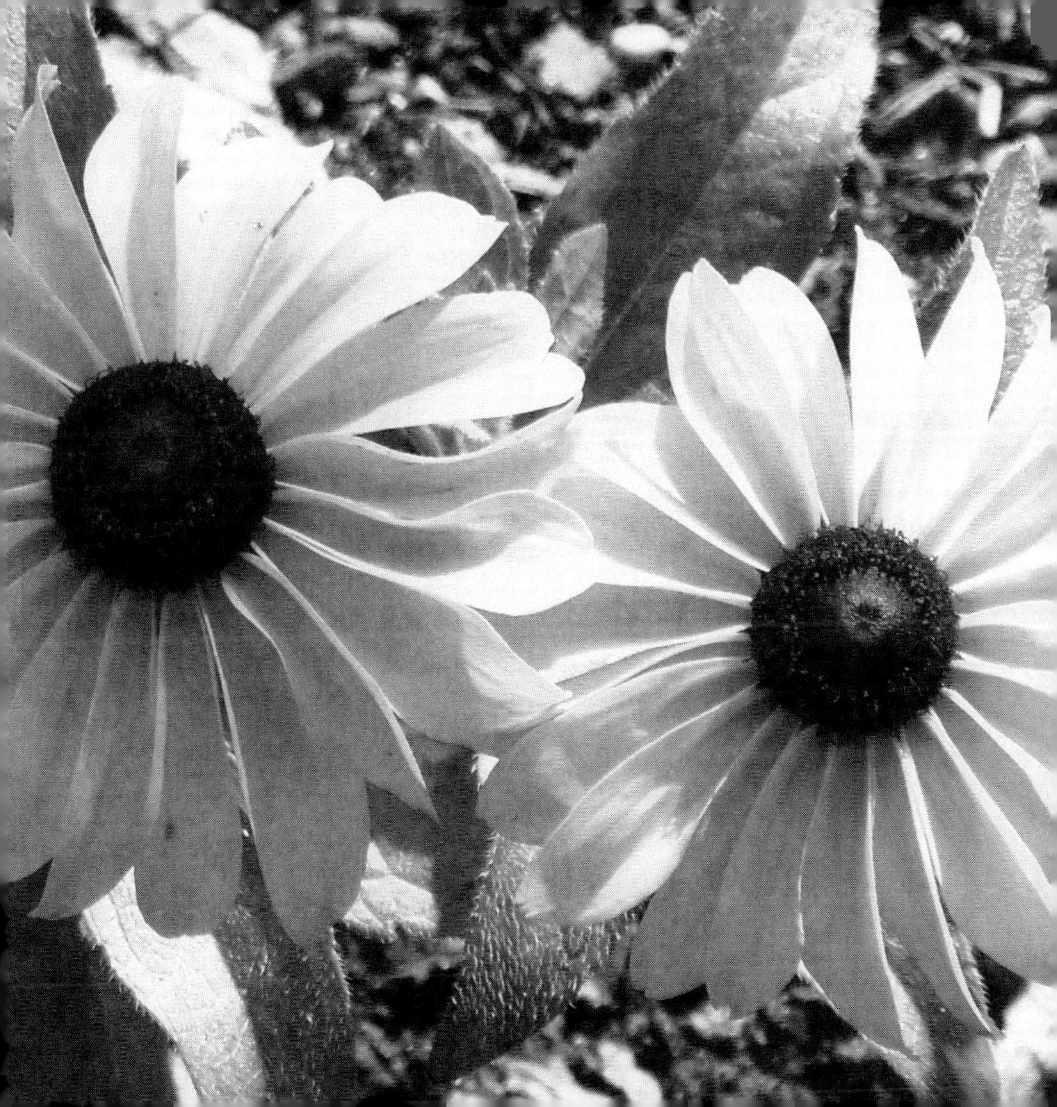

A Gift to a Charitable Organization

One night I was really upset about how greedy some people are. I could not fall asleep, and I was angry at a coworker who was complaining about universal health care. I stayed up until four in the morning and decided to do something positive with my anger. I decided then to give away all my earnings for the month of May to a charitable organization to sponsor a child. I did it as a gesture to show that greed is not in everybody. I did not spend any of the money on things that I did not need, such as clothing. I am now committed to doing this and sharing the idea with others. We need to make positive changes in our lives in order to change other people's lives.

**When we get out of our comfort zone, we grow.
Can you recall the feelings you had when you
gave the most to your favorite cause?**

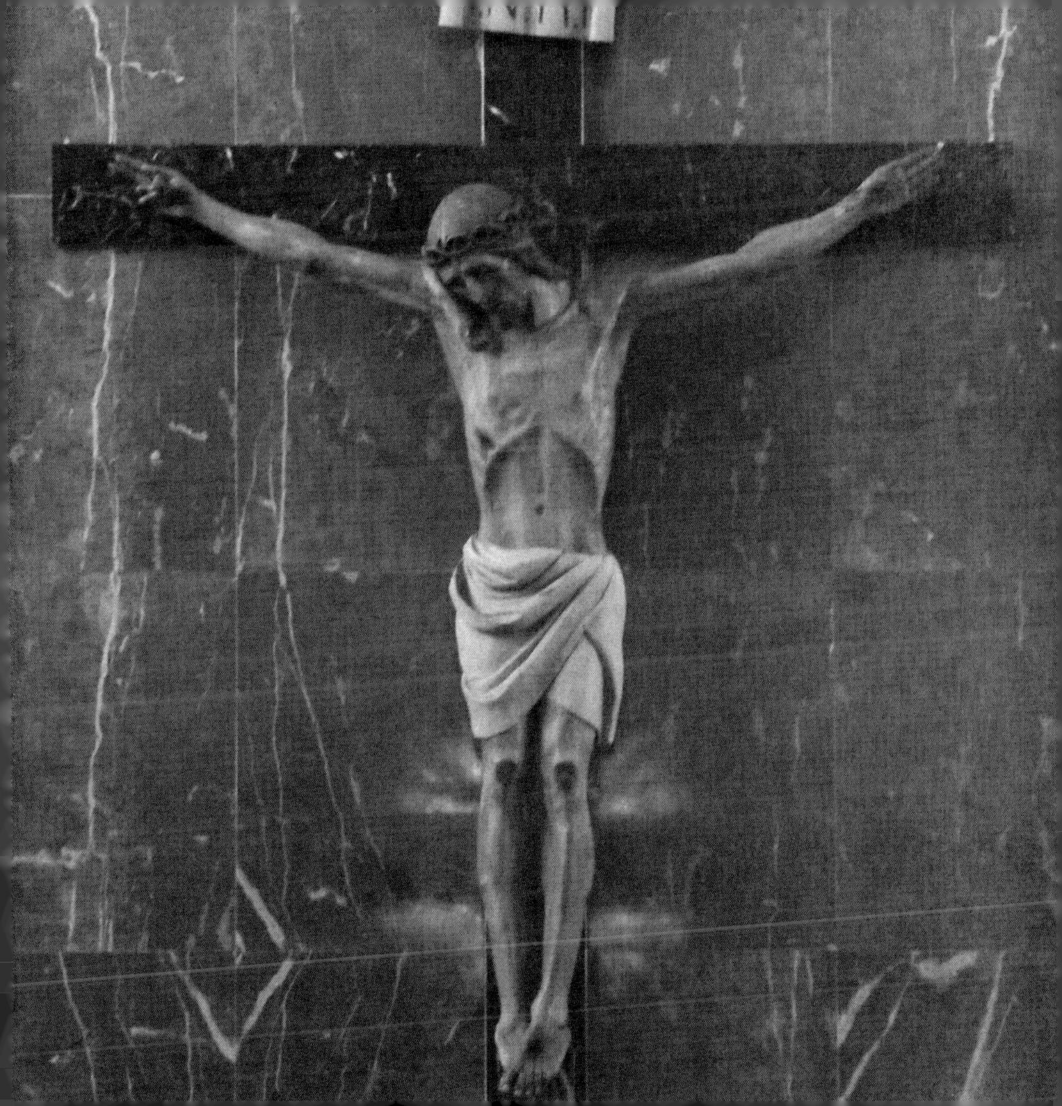

A Subway Ticket to Red Square in Moscow

On a sunny day back in the late 1970s when I was on a two-year assignment as an American military attaché in the Soviet Union, I went to Red Square to take some pictures. As I walked and photographed, I was struck by the symbolism of the four sides of the square. The past, present, and future of the Soviet Union was visible from the square center.

On one side is the Kremlin, the seat of power since the time of the Czars. Along the Kremlin wall is Lenin's tomb, guarded by Russian soldiers. Although long dead, he was still watching over the Soviet Union and communism. But just as the Kremlin was behind Lenin, it is the militarized state that preserves, even forces, communism. On the opposite side is GUM, the premier department store in the Soviet Union in a gleaming building with large picture windows that would fit in with the décor on 5th Avenue in New York City. Examining the inside of the store revealed nothing but shoddy goods that were not up to the quality of any local Salvation Army resale store. The store represents the false front on communism and socialism: to the naive it appears wonderful, but under scrutiny there is nothing but false promises.

On another corner is the museum dedicated to Lenin. Lenin was a criminal whose goal was evil control of the people. He had no intention of reducing the size of government over time, but rather, he desired to enslave all to the will of the state. Despite the facts, people were blinded, and he represents the false god of communism.

On the opposite side is St. Basil's Cathedral, or rather what is left of a major church perhaps ten times the size of the remnant. The remnant is what so many tourists and newscasters use as a background for Moscow reporting. It represents the true God. Although the communists do their best to foster atheism, faith in the state, and wipe out all vestiges of Christianity, they cannot do so. There is always a believing remnant.

As I was leaving Red Square, an overwhelming sense of anger came to me, and I realized then that the Soviet Union was doomed. I prayed the strongest prayer ever to God that He would destroy the Soviet Union. Faith then was new to me, and I was not even baptized yet! Once home, I called two ministers, one who was British and one who was American, and they came to my apartment, and right there, in my living room, they baptized me. I felt I had been hit with the truth, and the truth, which is Christ, set me free. From that day onward I committed my life to Christ. My commitment to Him is forever. For the past fifteen years I have been a servant for God's will, and I will continue to do good works for the rest of my life.

When stricken by truth, we can find ourselves.
When did you feel the presence of God
most strongly in your life?

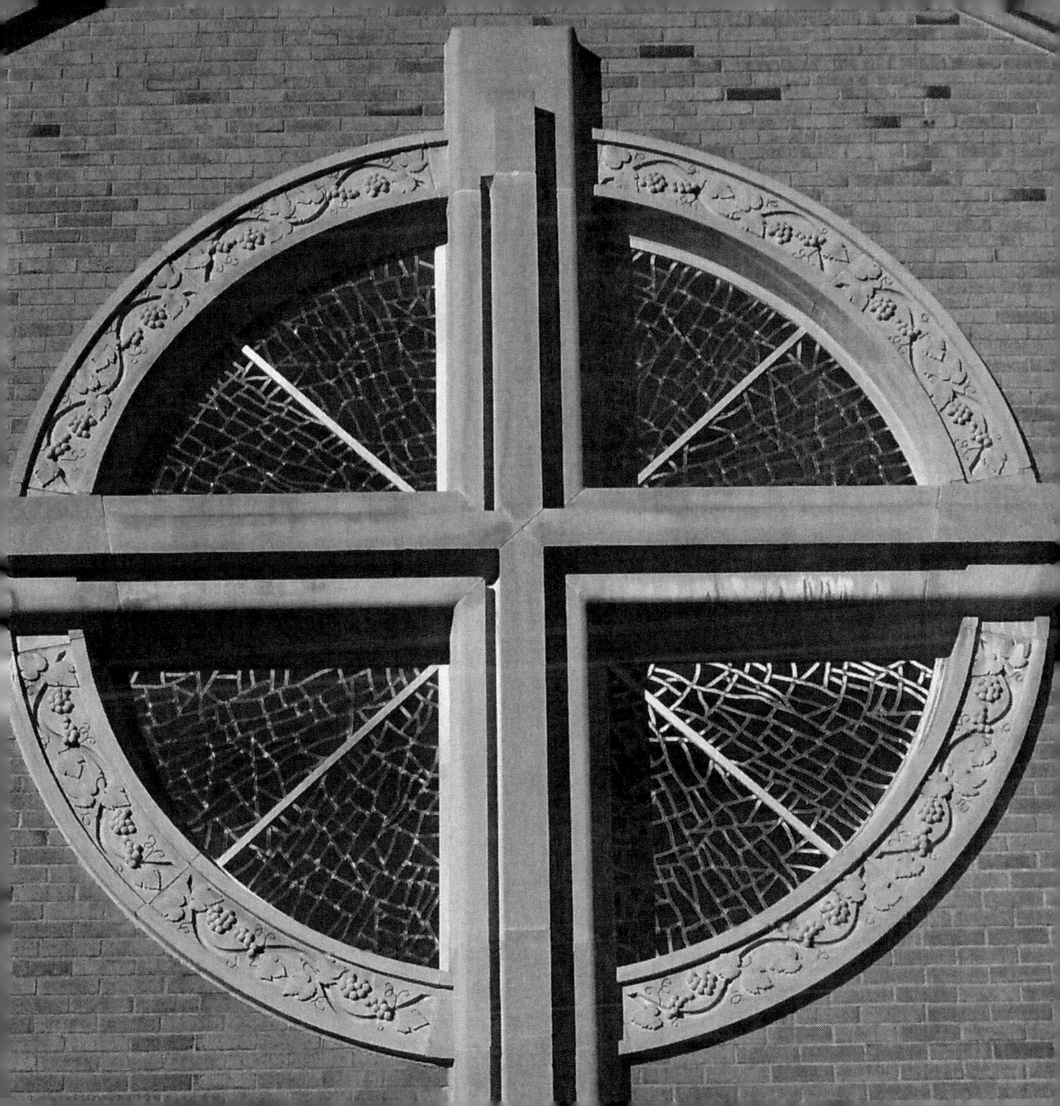

Taxes on a Ticket to Europe

When I was nineteen years old, my stepmother that worked for United Airlines out of Los Angeles gave me a ticket to go to Europe. I only had to pay for the taxes on the airfare ticket. I went for seventeen days with two friends and the book *The Birth of God* by Jean Bottero. We traveled to Holland, Denmark, England, and Germany. My two friends had Jewish ancestry, and they were very close, thus the reason for us to go to Germany.

We loved to play card games. My friends were so good at playing cards that they were the only ones I could not beat! The risk for me was landing at Heathrow Airport and finding my way to Gatwick Airport to find my friends. Otherwise, I was alone in Europe with $200.00. I kept a journal of the trip and also tape recorded. I often reflect on the trip and how it positively impacted my life. The trip changed my worldview. I saw how others lived, their sense of community, and life in the train stations. I also realized the value of friends and a good book. It also helped me to focus on college and to study history.

**Traveling to faraway lands sharpens our senses.
What lessons have you learned from traveling internationally?**

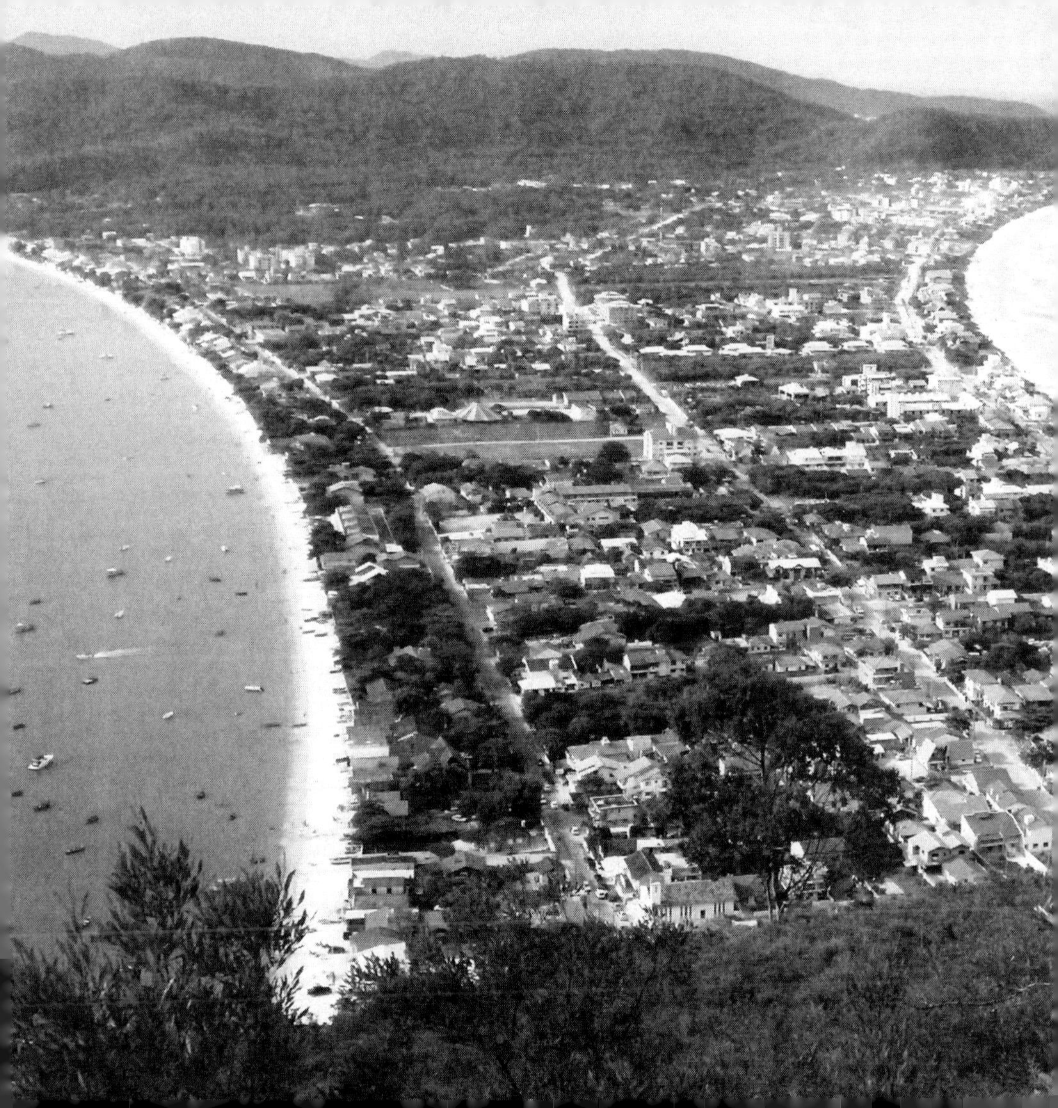

A College Application Fee

Upon finishing high school, I was not sure if I wanted to go to college. My family was lukewarm about me attending college at that time. Most of my friends were not going to college. I made the decision to apply to Western Michigan University using the few dollars that I had. I ended up loving the college experience, and I received my bachelor's degree in public health and went on to get my master's in public administration. It turned out to be a great decision since I love the work I do now in city management. College changed my whole perspective in life. It helped me to manage my schedule, become a reader, and start growing as a person. While in college, I started to understand better how the world operates. College also helped me to define the things I value in life, such as choosing the right place to live so I can provide the best environment for my family and the education of our children.

**Choose carefully where to build a life to bear your fruit.
What influenced you most in your choice
of which college to attend?**

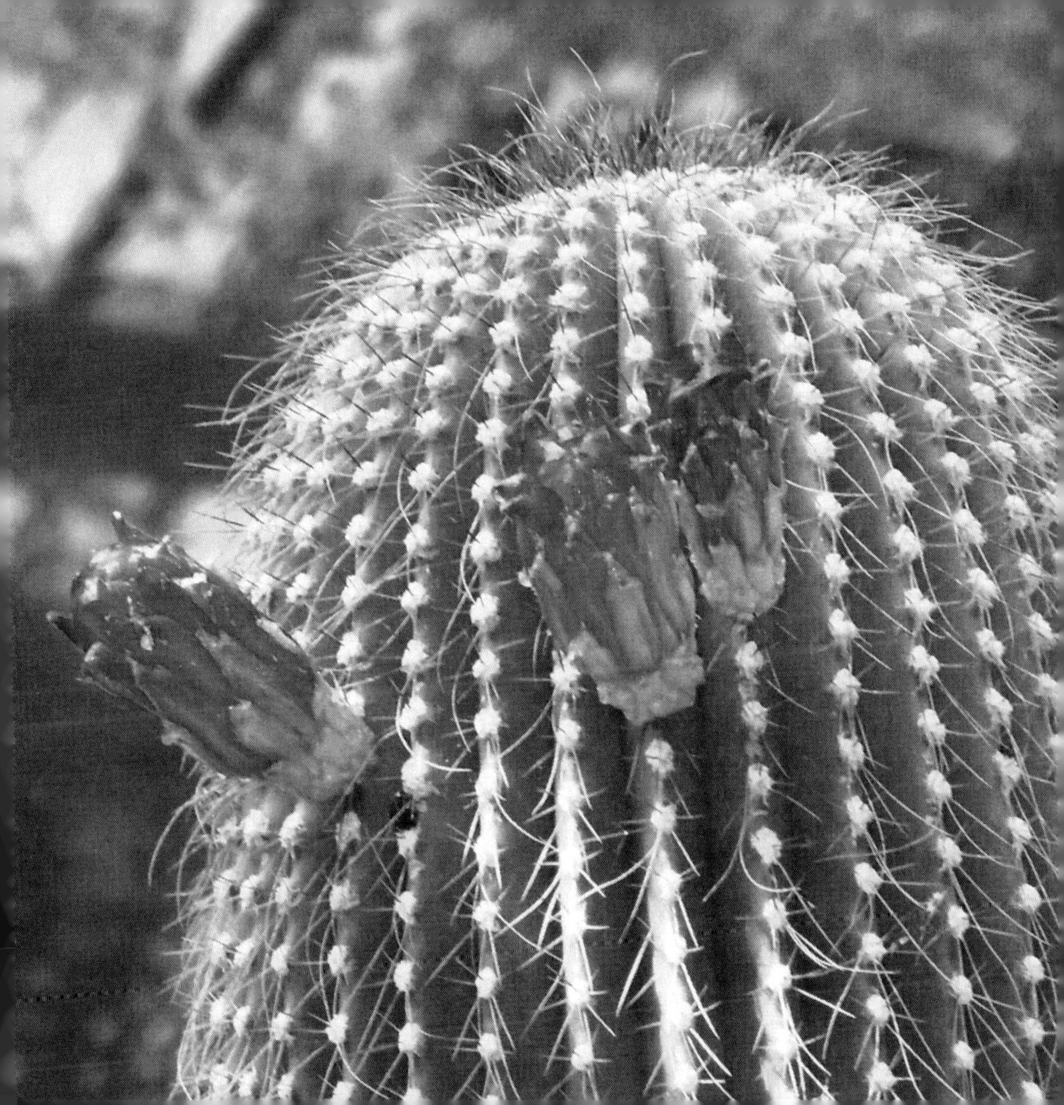

A Midnight Breakfast

I had been on a quest to find out what "truth" was for over a year, which led to me searching and reading book after book. After reading a number of religious books, I decided that maybe I needed to go on a fast to help get my answer. I decided to start a three-day water-only fast, and to make things really spiritual I would only watch Christian TV. I have to admit that not eating anything for three days was not easy! Besides the general weakness I felt after the first day, I was starving. Yet I held on to my commitment.

Peering anxiously at my watch every few minutes, I decided that I would go to the drive-thru at Burger King right at the stroke of midnight to break my fast. I pulled up, placed my order, and after paying my nearly $10 fast food bill, I drove off stuffing French Fries in my mouth like the starving creature I was! You might have seen this coming, but it is not a good idea to stuff this much fast food into a stomach that has been empty for three days!

Shortly after a nearly sleepless night of struggling to digest all that food, I woke up to watch a television program I had discovered while fasting from secular television. The show was *Success-N-Life*... with a by-line *With Jesus Christ*. As I listened to the program, I found that everyone has sinned in some way and that we are all separated from God but that there was good news. Jesus had done something for us that restored the relationship that I had lost with God. But what did He do?

Jesus lived a sinless life, and because He was pure, He could pay the price for those of us who were not. And even though He had never done anything wrong in His life, He allowed Himself to be killed on our behalf. I had never heard this before! You mean to tell me that I could have a completely restored relationship with God by believing in what Jesus did on my behalf? I got down on my knees and prayed with the television preacher, "God, I am sorry for doing the things that I have done that were not pleasing to you and that separated us. I want to thank you for sending your son to pay my penalty. And because of your favor that I do not deserve and your mercy, I can enter into a new relationship with you through faith alone—not earning a thing, but simply believing. Thank you. I accept it!"

It was amazing. I knew that I was forgiven. I knew that I would spend all eternity with my Lord and Savior and that I did nothing to deserve it. It was a gift of love from God! Even though this transformation took place over twenty years ago, I will never forget my $10 "breakfast" and the life-changing things that trans pired shortly after. I now love God more than ever. I now live my life with as much appreciation as I can muster every day. I sincerely hope that everyone hears about what this incredible God, who is love, has done for us!

**Moments of truth are powerful.
How often do you reflect on something
that changed you forever?**

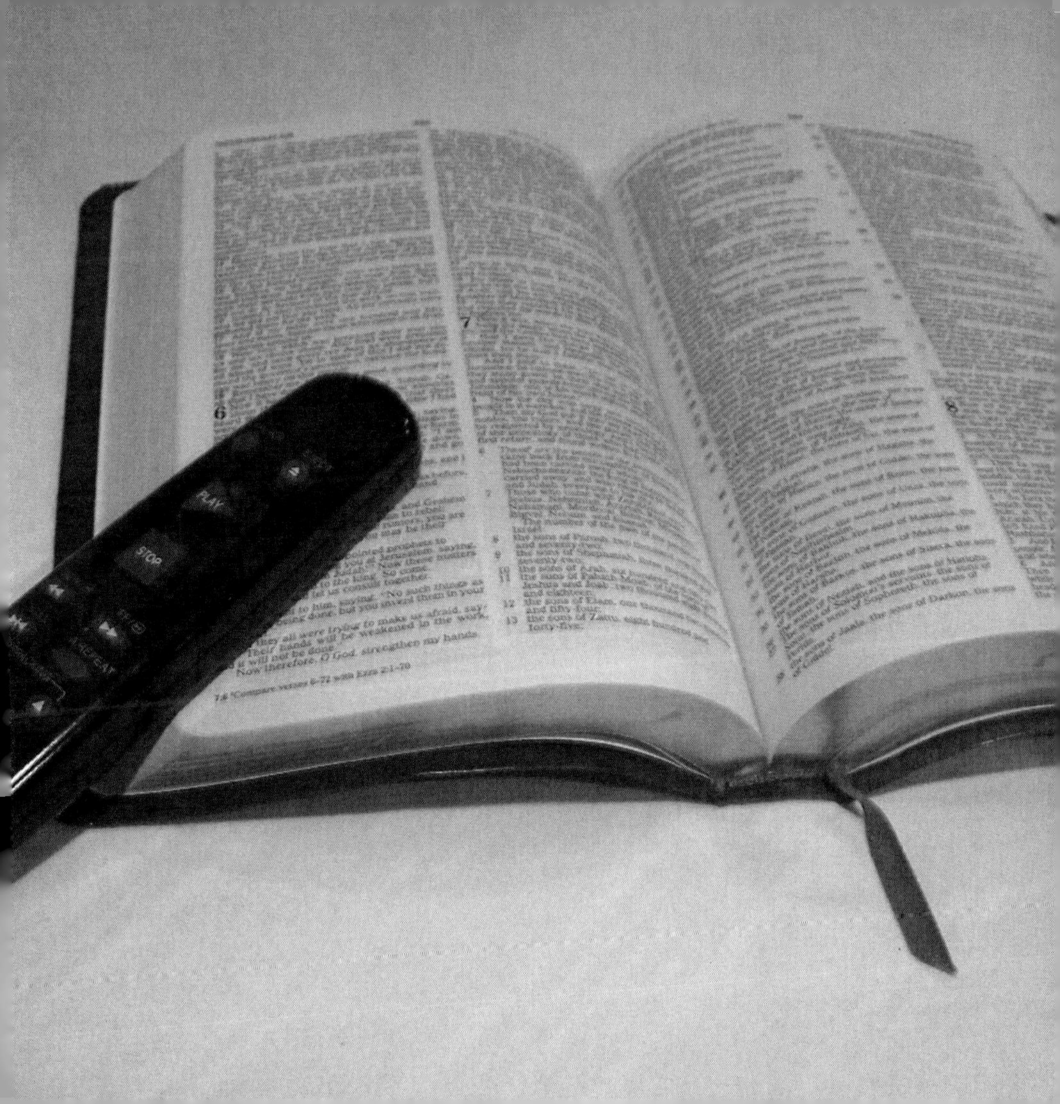
PLAY
STOP
REPEAT

STORIES OF LOVE

Money for the
Church Collection Basket

The best value I ever got for about $10 was the money I put into the collection basket at my church. I have received so many blessings and have an abundant life, so it is a great feeling to be able to give to my church. I believe givers receive more than they give. Go out and give of yourself—not just money, but also of your time and talents to help those in need!

Blessings come from giving.
How do you feel after you count your blessings?

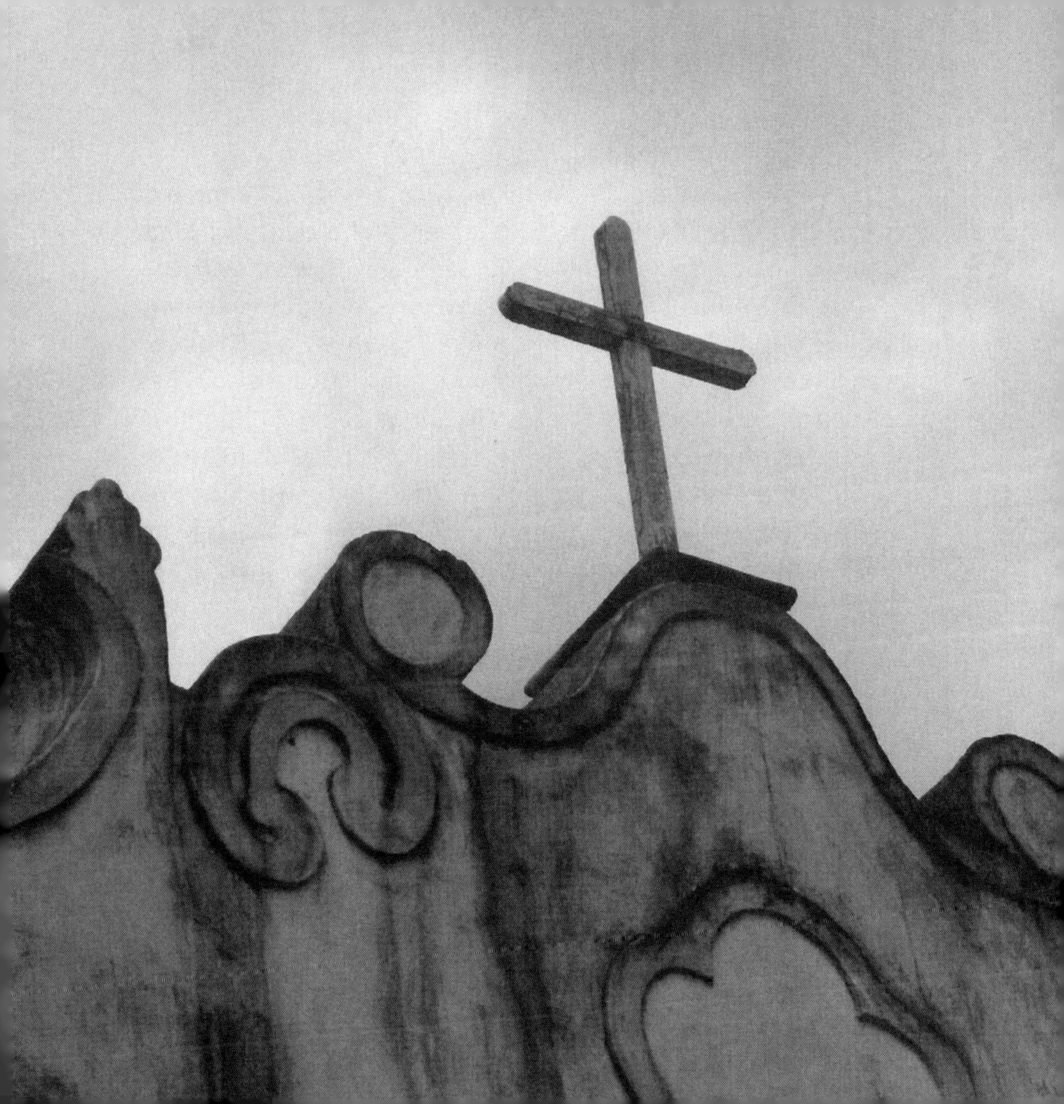

A Marriage License

Our marriage license was a small investment that made the biggest impact in my life. It was the beginning of a new and great life. It was the beginning of the life I dreamed of. It was a new reality for me and for us. Today I have a hard time even remembering life before our marriage. Yes, there are times when he gets on my nerves, times that I want to strangle him, but there are also times of immense joy in living with him. He brings so much humor to life and to our lives. His personality is so different than mine. He is an extrovert, and I am the opposite, an introvert. He is so full of energy. I love to hear him laughing, which is a normal state for him. He is so loving and so giving, and I always feel that he can do anything for me and for us. It has been an incredible journey, worth every step and every detour.

True love is pure, patient, and persistent.
What do you do to keep your crucial loving relationships alive?

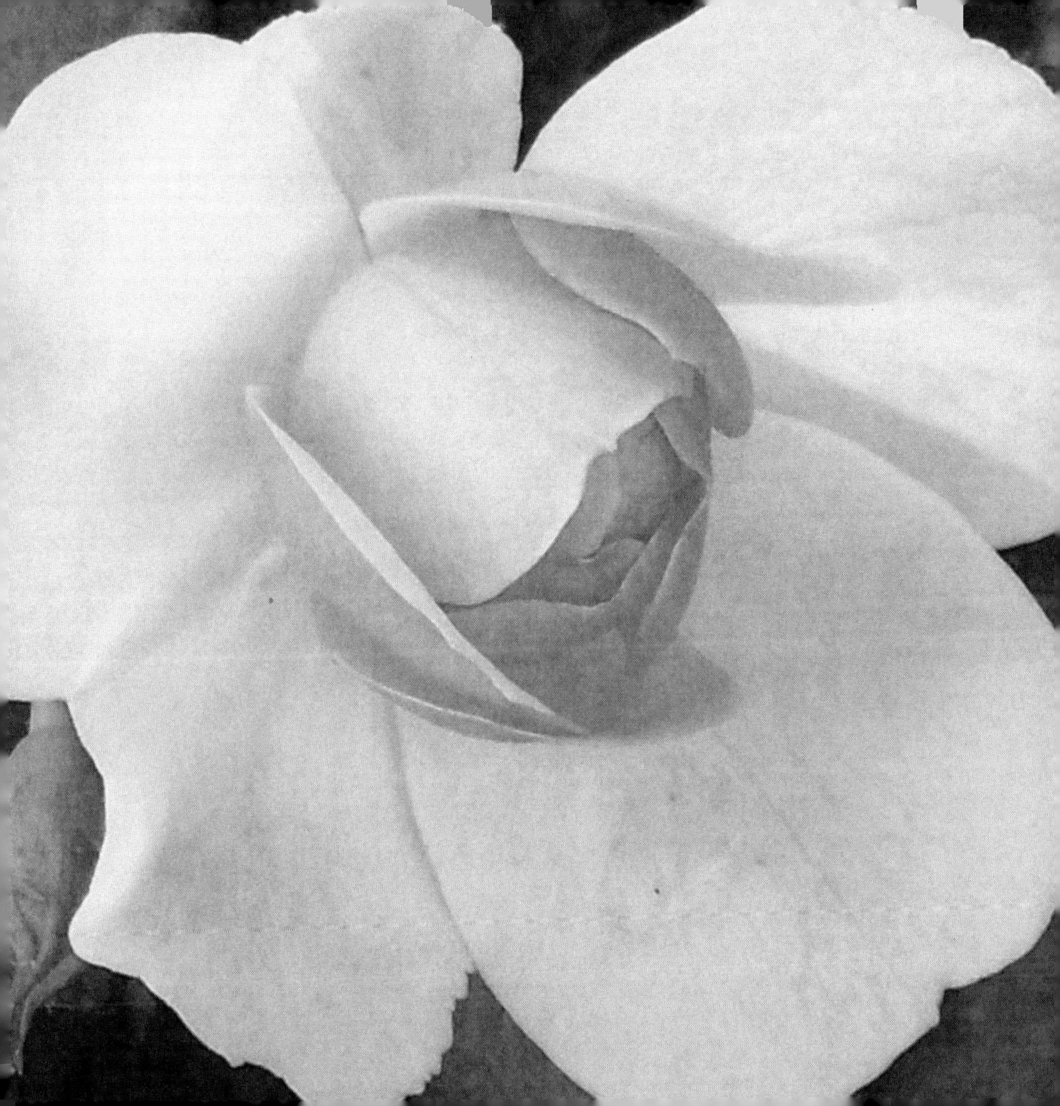

A Basket of Flowers

The best thing I ever bought was a basket of flowers for a friend. Why? The flowers made my friend smile. Flowers make people smile. People appreciate beauty. When I give people flowers, it makes them feel valued and appreciated. That is why my favorite gift to give is flowers. I love to see people smile!

Appreciation for beauty leads to happiness. What kinds of reactions do you receive when you give people something beautiful?

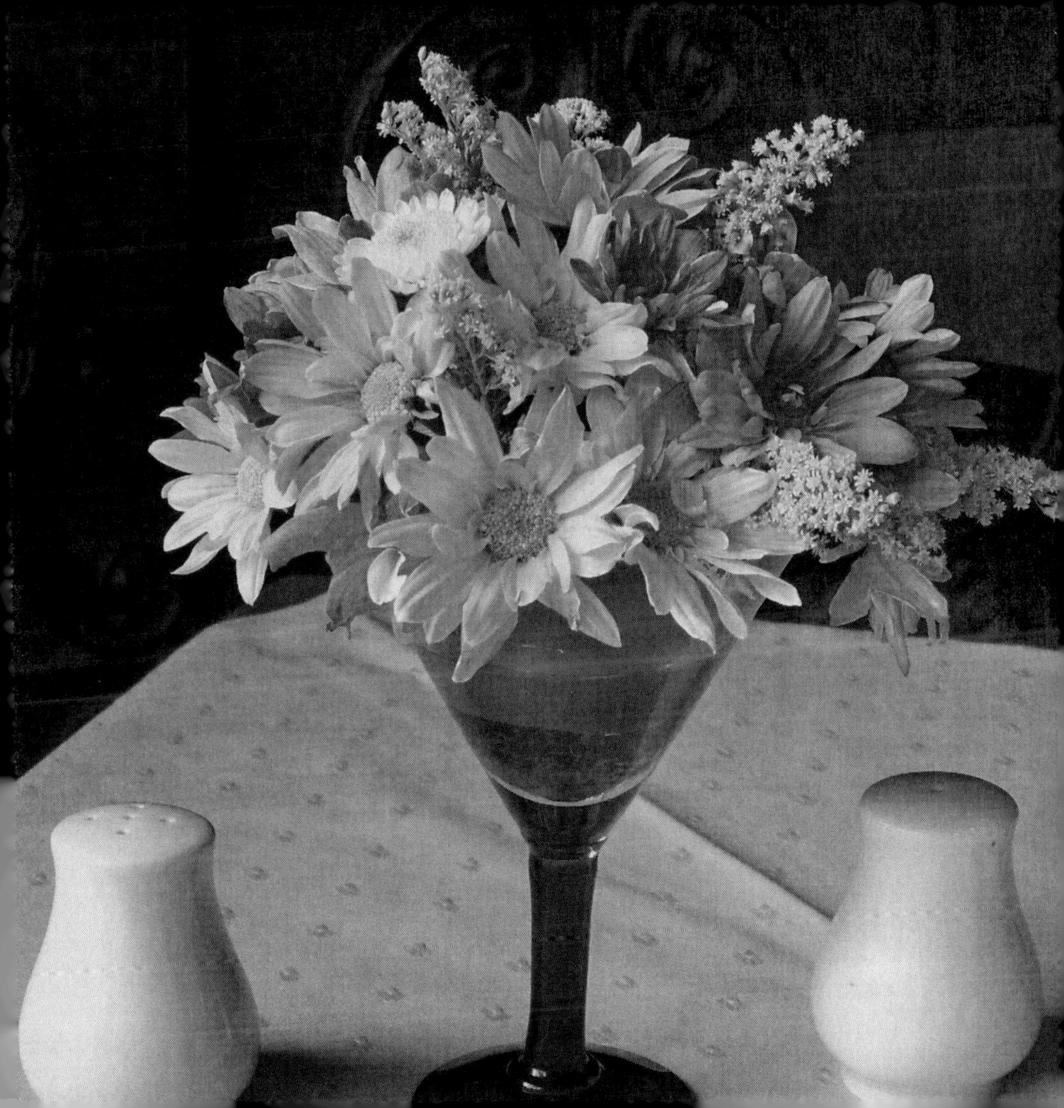

A Bag of Candy

When I was in high school, I spent about $10 to buy a big bag of suckers to take with me on a trip to Mexico. Once there, I passed out suckers to small children in a poor village in Monterey. It was incredible how such a small and fun gift opened up the doors to friendships. Small things mean a lot for those who have so little! I have never forgotten that lesson. We are so fortunate to live in a society of plenty that we forget that most of the people in the world have so little to live with.

**People's hearts are more similar than their outer appearances.
How do you share your prosperity with
those less fortunate than you?**

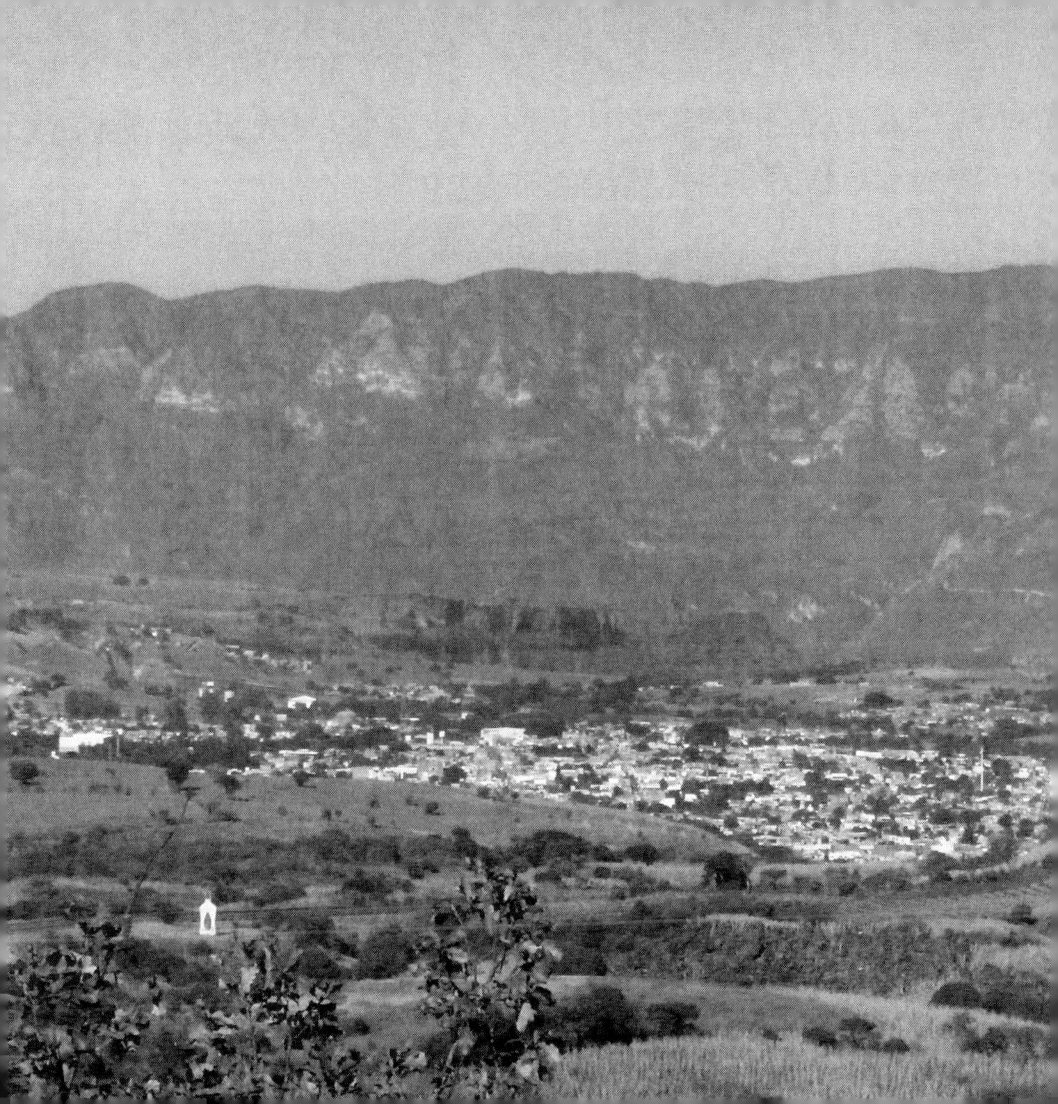

Magnifying Glasses

A few years ago I spent about $10 to buy magnifying glasses for a man that was losing his eyesight. The glasses were important to him because he loved to read. This little gift gave him back the joy of reading. I learned that it is the simple things that can make a big difference in someone's life. There are so many opportunities for us to help others; we just need to be observant and learn to ask the right questions so we can find out what the little things missing in peoples' lives are. There is so much more we can do when we put serving others as a priority!

God's creations are magnificent.
How do you go about discovering the needs of others?

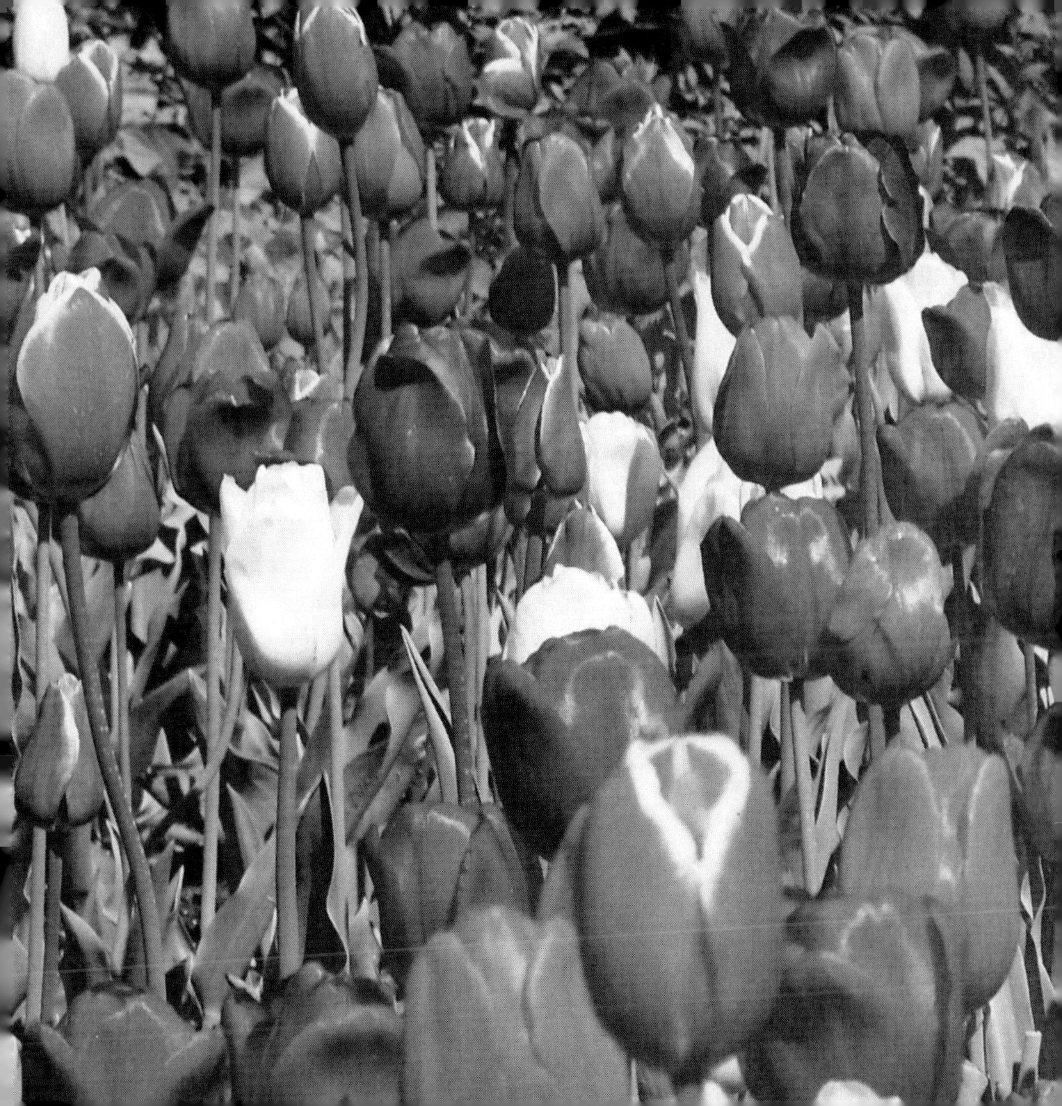

Towing a Stranger's Car

A few years ago while I was taking a walk on Christmas evening, I saw someone stranded on the side of the road. I stopped and asked if they needed help. They were having car trouble and had no means to get home, so I paid for the tow truck to take their car home. I was very young, and I did not have much money at that time. I gave them all the money I had, and it felt so wonderful to help someone in need. I think true giving is about giving all we have, not just the extra, with no expectation of receiving something in return. It sure feels great to remember that I helped someone in need on a Christmas evening.

When we help others, we help ourselves.
Are you willing to inconvenience yourself
to bring convenience to others?

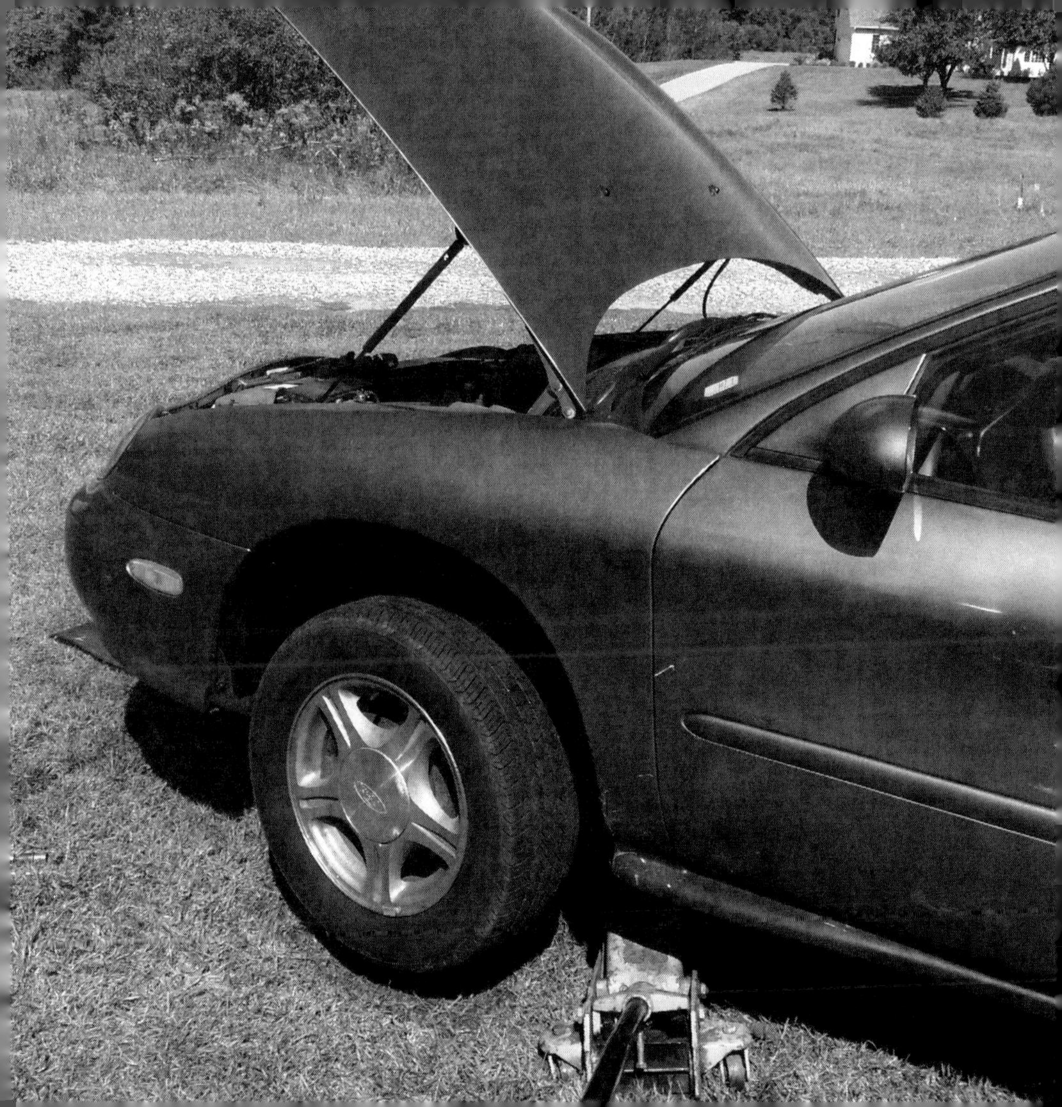

Groceries for Those Who Can't Afford Them

The best money I have ever spent was to help strangers pay for their groceries at supermarket checkouts. Helping people in need is very important to me. I like to pay it forward and to give anonymously. It is so rewarding to help those in need, especially in this tough economy. I always make it a habit of being on the lookout for those in need now, not later!

Giving always comes before receiving.
How does giving change the heart of the giver?

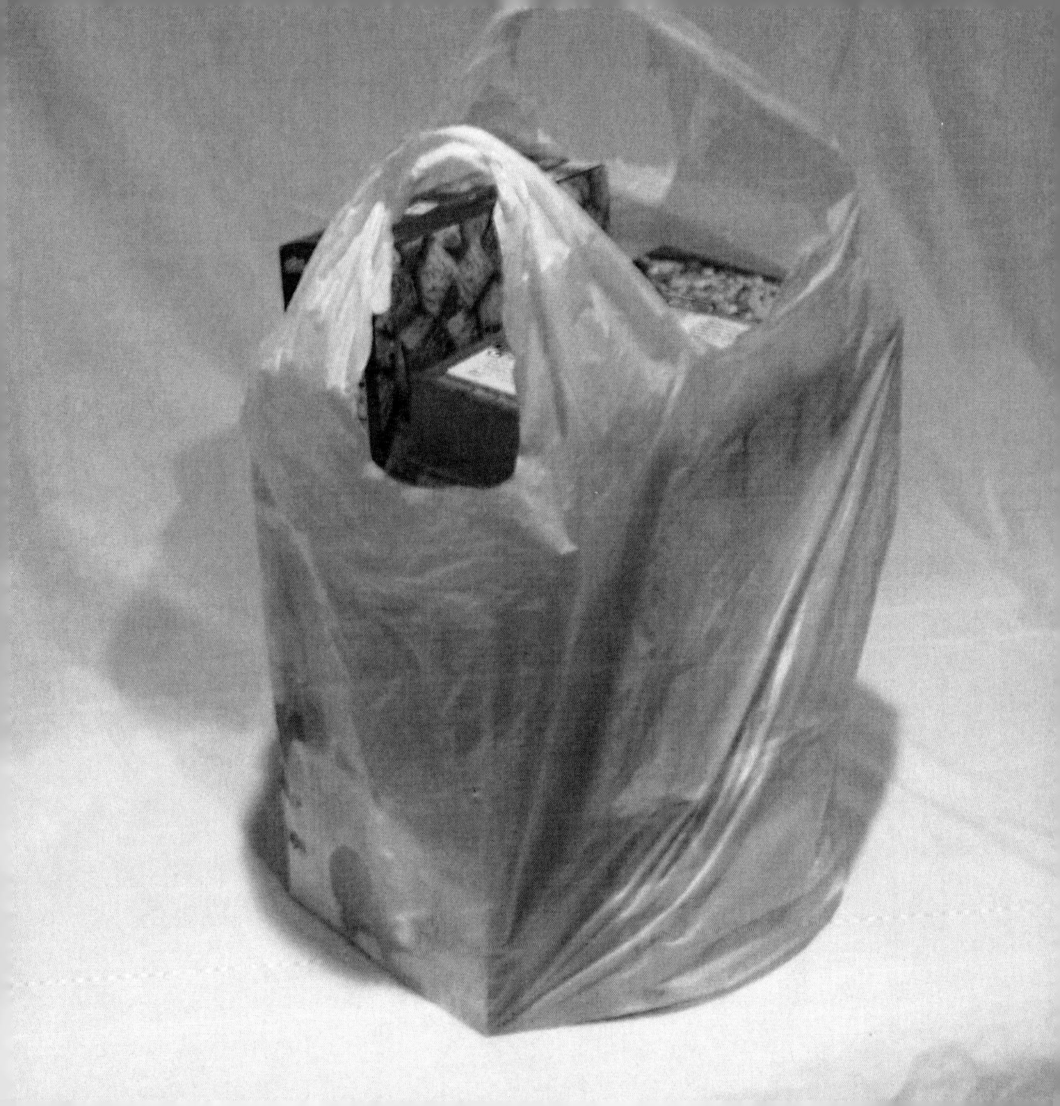

Letter Writing Supplies

Years ago I bought a pen, envelope, paper, and stamps to write personal letters to my parents and my siblings. I found it was easier to express my feelings in words than in person, so I wrote to each of my family members on their birthdays. I would write about what each one of them meant to me. I wrote to them in case something were to ever happen to me, or to them, so that each one would know how I felt about them. I am so glad I did this because both of my parents have now passed away. Writing is very powerful and liberating for both the writer and the reader. It is also easier for us to accept since we can have privacy with our feelings. This action took a load off my mind, and I felt great about doing it. I highly recommend that everyone do this as well!

Express love often to your dear ones.
How have you expressed to your loved
ones what they mean to you?

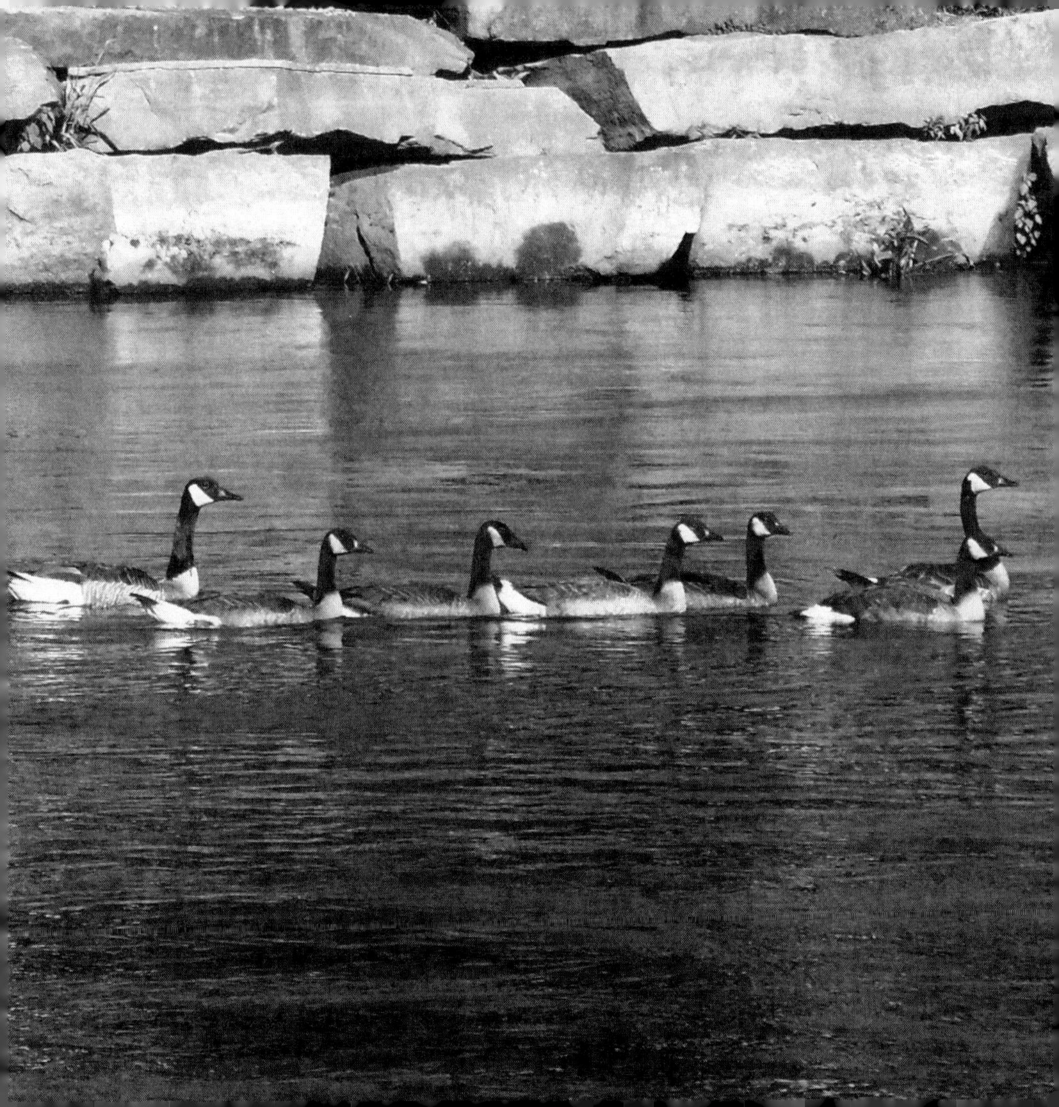

A Meal for a Homeless Man

I bought a large coffee and meal for a homeless man in the middle of the winter a few years ago. The man was inside a sandwich shop getting warm during a very cold winter day in Michigan. I started the conversation by having small talk.

"Cold out there, isn't it?"

"Yes, bitter cold," he said.

Then, I said, "I am not much of a coffee drinker, but how is the coffee here?"

"Pretty good," he said.

I told him that I had some coupons I likely would not use. "Would you like me to get you a sandwich and a large coffee?" I asked him. I just wanted him to know that the meal was not going to cost me anything. He said yes, and I sensed he needed someone to talk to more than he needed the meal. We talked, and we both felt great about the whole experience!

The best gift of all is the gift of self.
When was the last time you went out of your
way to help someone else in need?

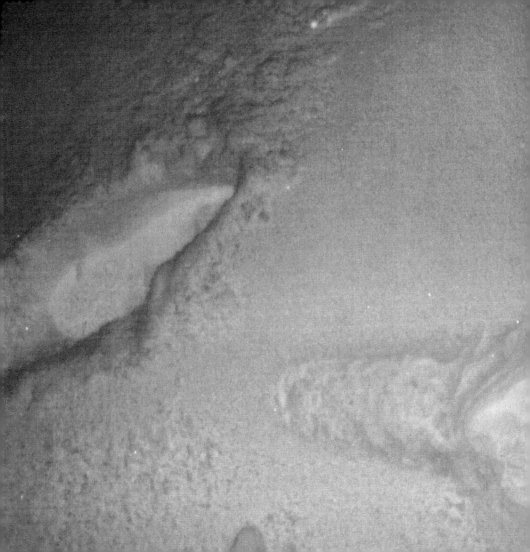

A Train Ticket for My Son

The best money I ever spent would probably be the Amtrak ticket I bought for my son to take the train instead of relying on his mom or dad to drive him from Kalamazoo to East Lansing, Michigan. He was skeptical about trying something new, but this helped him break out of his shell a little bit and know that he could do things on his own. It is part of helping your kids get launched. I look for those opportunities. Later, he spent a summer in London and has now moved to San Diego and is successfully creating a life for himself out west.

Private victories come before public victories. Why shouldn't you do for others what they can do for themselves?

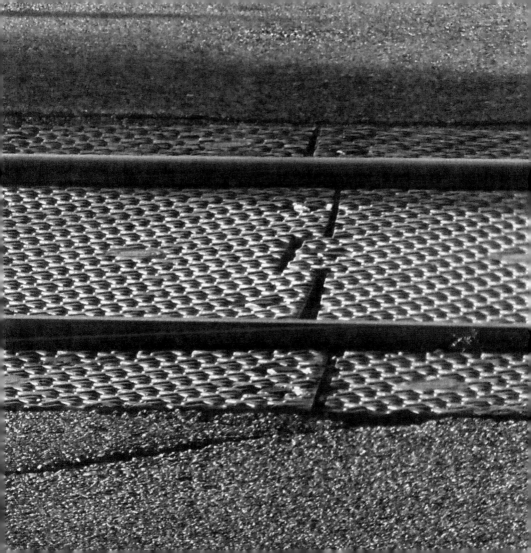

A Christmas Present for My Mother

Well, this story did not cost me anything. Christmas was coming, and I was about eight years old. I wanted to get my mom something she really wanted. I did not have any money and had no way of making any. So with that, what could I do? My mom had a favorite belt she just loved. One day I got in her drawer and took the belt and wrapped it up for a Christmas present. How could I go wrong? She would love the belt. I was so excited, and every time that my mom looked for that belt, I would giggle to myself, knowing where it was and how excited she would be on Christmas morning to open it up and find it. Christmas morning came, and when she opened it, I couldn't stand the suspense. She was so excited and told me I couldn't have given her a better gift. I was so happy. We tell that story over and over and get the biggest laugh out of it. Many years have passed since that Christmas, and Mom is gone now, but the story has become a family story to pass down through the years. Having money just wasn't the answer; it was figuring out what to do when I didn't have any.

Natural beauty can be ephemeral.
Why do the priceless moments in life
cost so little or nothing at all?

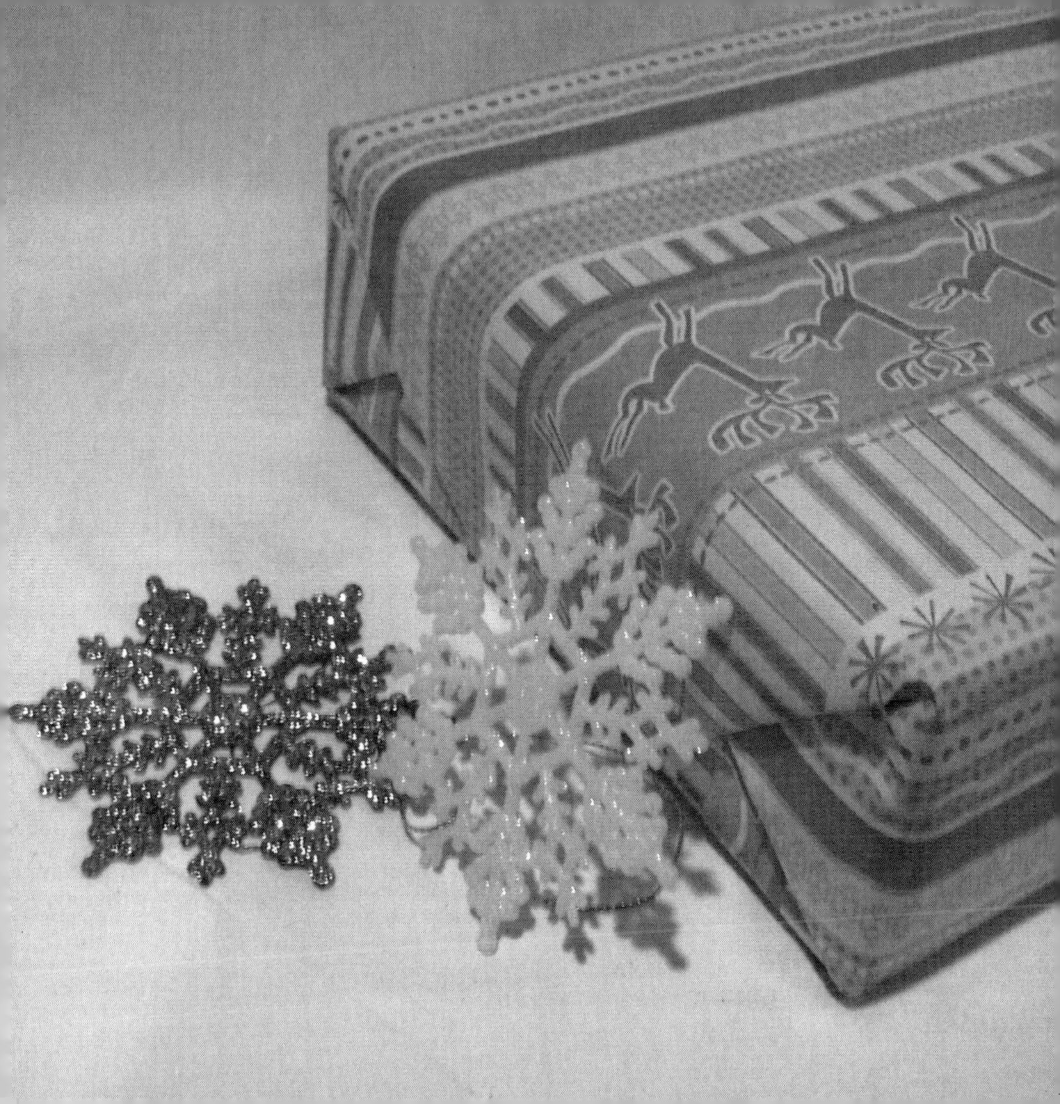

Milk and Bread

When I was thirteen years old, my dad's employment required us to spend a summer in the Philippines. The company put us up in one of the nicest neighborhoods in Manila and provided us with a maid, a driver, and a house boy. It was a great experience, and I soon became friends with many kids in the area. Every week-end the driver would take us sightseeing. We saw many beautiful sights, but we also saw a lot of poverty. Each day fresh milk and bread were delivered to our house and placed in a basket just inside the gate. All of the houses in this neighborhood had deco-rative fences around them, primarily to keep snakes and large monitor lizards out, but I suspect to also separate them from the poverty only a few hundred yards away.

Partway through the summer, our milk and bread were some-times not in the basket when our house boy showed up in the morning. The house boy started coming to the house early to wait for the deliveries. The milk and bread were delivered each morn-ing, but one morning the house boy noticed someone sneaking along the fence row. He deduced that someone, probably this person sneaking just outside our fence, was stealing the milk and bread. He rushed into our house looking for a bat or something to "beat up" this robber. My dad was inside getting ready to go into work, and upon learning what was going on, he forbid the house boy from taking action. He told the house boy, and later the rest of our family, that even though it is wrong to steal, this person clearly needed this food more than we did, and it appeared that he was only taking what he needed to survive. This is just one of many lessons I have learned from my father and about life.

There is something uncommon about
common fresh bread and milk.
What is the most memorable travel story in your life?

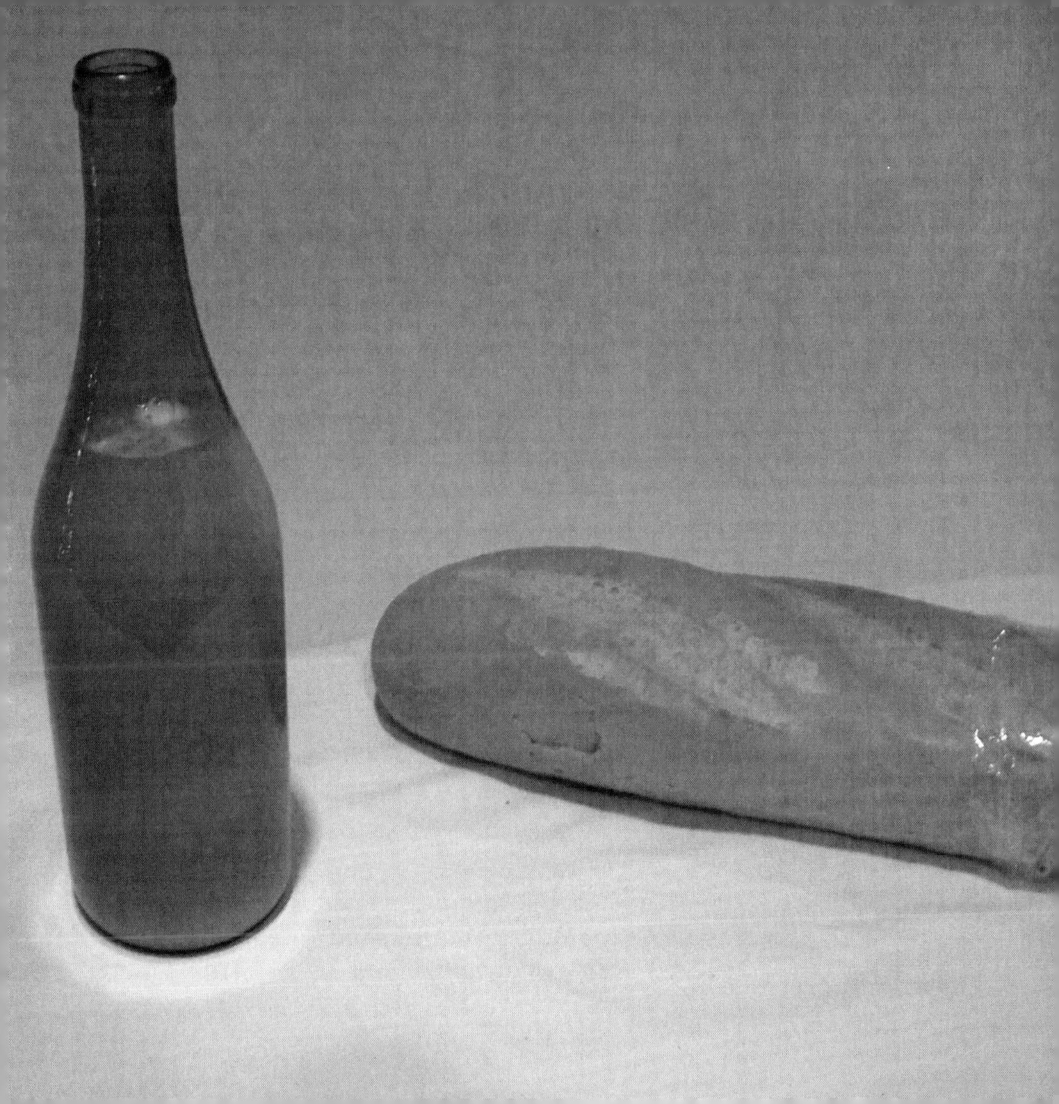

Josh Groban *Noel* CD

While my grandmother was in her last days in Hospice, we were trying to bring a little joy to such a sorrowful time during the holidays. She was there in December, and we sat by her bed every day trying to prepare her for her next journey in life. It was sad that there was so much sadness when we were supposed to be celebrating the birth of Christ, and she was "missing" it all. So, I thought I would bring Christmas to her anyway I could. I went and bought the Josh Groban *Noel* CD, loaded it on my iPod, and put the headphones in her ear, on low. She hadn't responded to us in days, but when the music played quietly in her ear, she looked peaceful and squeezed my hand for the last time. From that moment I realized how powerful music can be, especially the song "Silent Night?" As she listened, I was praying that she would "sleep in heavenly peace." Since that day, now I listen to "Silent Night" with a totally different mind-set, and I know that there can be peace in death. I constantly replay "sleep in heavenly peace" in my head and know that she is among the angels and sits by God.

Seasons come and go, but memories last forever.
What important memories are triggered when
you listen to your favorite song?

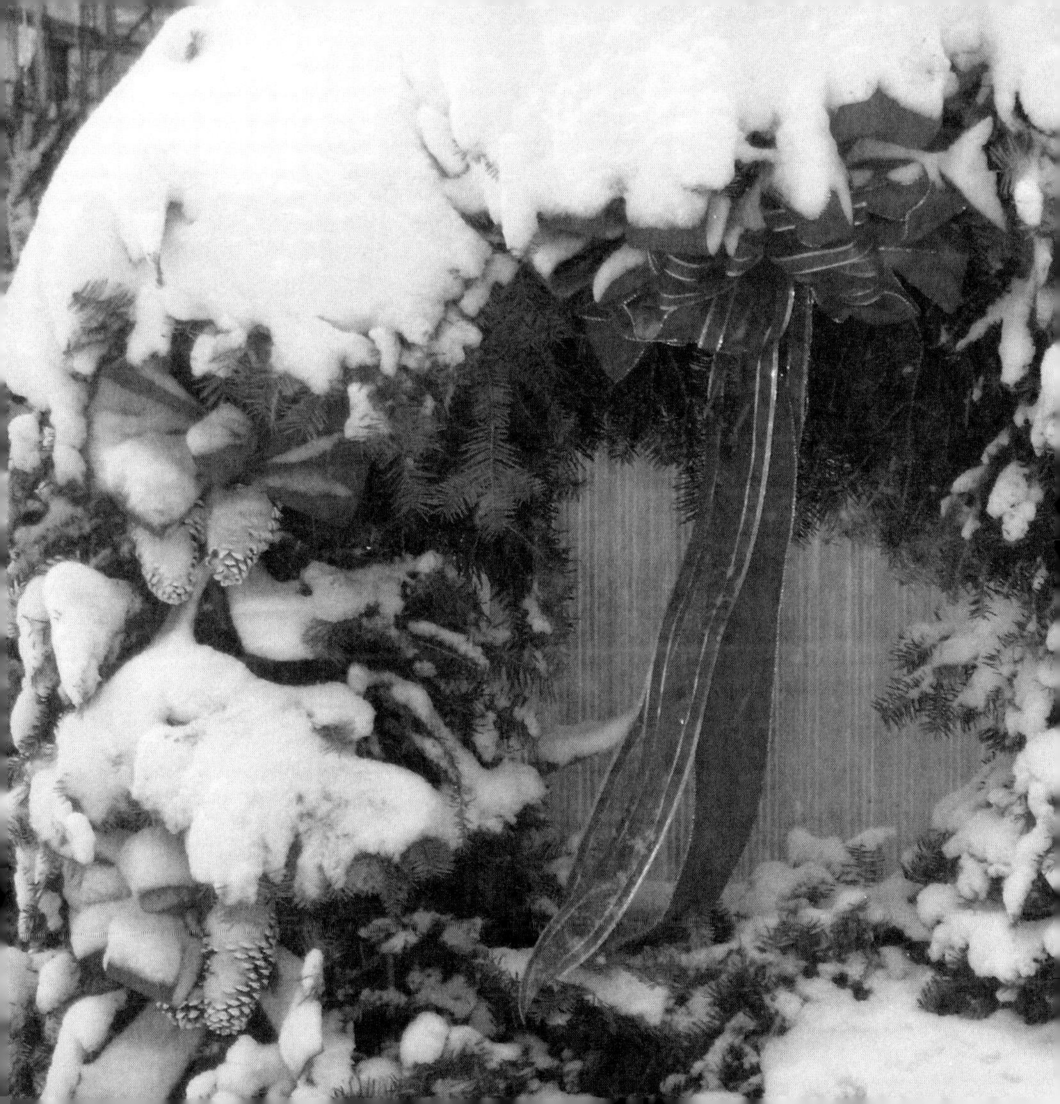

A Raffle Ticket

I am a big outdoorsman, and I especially love trout fishing. So does my older son, who was living in Georgia at the time after finishing college down there and getting married. He has been my "fishing buddy" since he was a little kid. My wife and I were invited to a sportsman's banquet sponsored by Trout Unlimited, of which I am a member. At this banquet, the club was raffling off a very special bamboo fly rod that had been made here in Michigan around 1950 by a famous rod builder named Paul Young who was deceased. It was given to the club by the widow of the original owner. Tickets for the raffle were $20 each, and I bought one when we arrived, hoping I would win the rod, which was worth a lot of money but, more importantly, was a great collection piece.

The night went on, and several hours later they announced one last call for raffle tickets. I wondered to myself if I should call my son to see if he would want to buy a ticket. I thought better of it though since he had little extra cash to spend on something like this. Instead, I decided that I would buy a ticket for him. I remember that I didn't even have the $20. I only had $10 in my wallet. So I gave it to the guy with the tickets and said I would find my wife and get the other $10 from her, which I did at the last second. On both of the tickets I had purchased, I wrote my son's name. I went back to my seat and not more than thirty seconds later they did the ticket drawing. He pulled out the ticket and announced that my son had won the Paul Young rod! I couldn't believe it since I never win anything.

After some of the excitement calmed down, I told my wife that I was going to give the rod to our son. I called him up and told him that his name was drawn in the raffle and he was now the proud owner of the Paul Young rod. He thought I was kidding, but my wife and other people at our table got on the phone and con-firmed it. I could hear the whooping and hollering on the other end of the phone, which brought tears of joy to my eyes. That rod was assessed for $3,300, and I was able to give that to my son, who I love very much, to bring some happiness to him. He has not forgotten that, and we still talk about the strange circum-stances and luck of the draw to this day. I could have kept that rod since I bought both tickets, but it was far more rewarding to be unselfish and give it to my son.

We are remembered more by what
we give than by what we receive.
What experiences of self-sacrifice have
impacted your life the most?

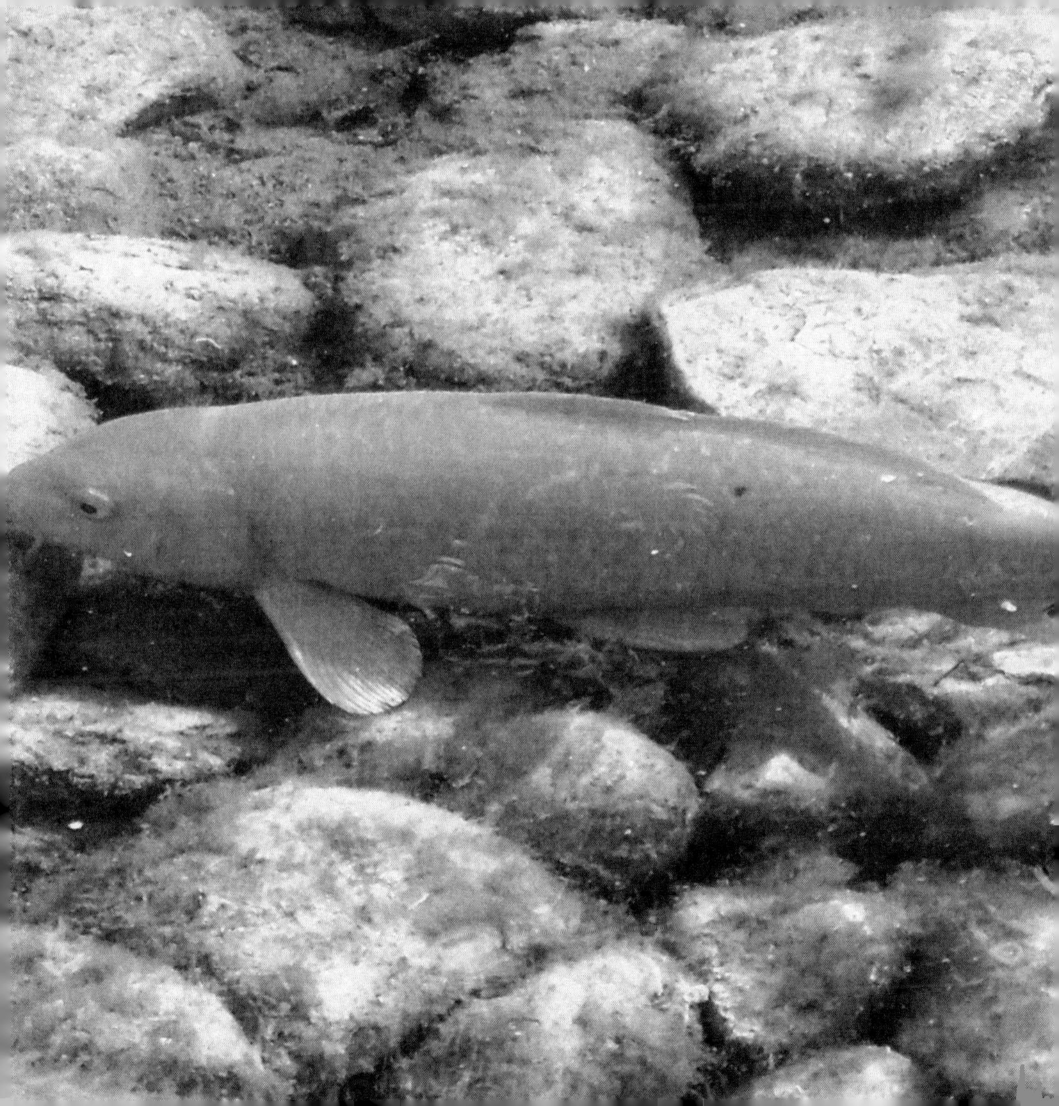

Dinner at a Restaurant

My wife and I were going to enjoy a show at the Performing Arts Center, San Juan's premiere entertainment venue in Puerto Rico. Before the show, we stopped at a nearby restaurant for dinner. While entering the restaurant, we were approached by a very young couple in their early twenties. They asked us for spare change to eat dinner. They looked dirty and weak, especially the woman, who also looked thin and sick. She was leaning on him and couldn't hide ugly lacerations on both of her legs. He shared with us that they were both homeless and had AIDS.

Their families threw them out on the street when they learned about their illness. They said they were sorry to beg for food, but they were very hungry and were not getting much money from people. There was no way we would enjoy a meal or a show if we turned our backs or if we just handed them our spare change. I invited them to join us for dinner. Their expression changed twice within very few seconds. They were pleasantly surprised by the offer, but their faces quickly showed concern.

He shared that the restaurant management would not let them near the door. As if they were queued, an employee approached us, yelling at the couple to go away and stop bothering the customers. I quickly intervened and told her that we welcomed their approach. The young man asked if we could order take out for them. The employee quickly stated that they couldn't come into the restaurant, not even to read the menu. Answering my question, she agreed to have me bring a menu to them but asked that they didn't touch it, and if they did, they should toss it into the garbage when finished. Only a few times in my life have I seen the expression of gratitude that I saw in their faces when receiving the food.

Before they slowly disappeared into the night, I asked how often they frequented the area, hoping to feed them again. But we all knew that they wouldn't last long. In spite of my good intentions, we all sort of knew that this was the first and last time that we would meet. I was overwhelmed by the moment and cried loudly, publicly into my wife's shoulder in the middle of the building's lobby. She helped me move to a secluded corner of the lobby until I regained composure several minutes later.

I don't remember too many times in my life when I have cried that loudly. I never saw them again. It's been roughly fifteen years since that encounter, but I remember them and get inspired by them very often. Before that day, my wife would shy away from similar approaches when she was out by herself, but honoring this experience she has chosen to help. I continue to help every single time, always thinking of them.

There is depth in the beauty of every human soul.
What comes to your mind when you see
homeless people on the streets?

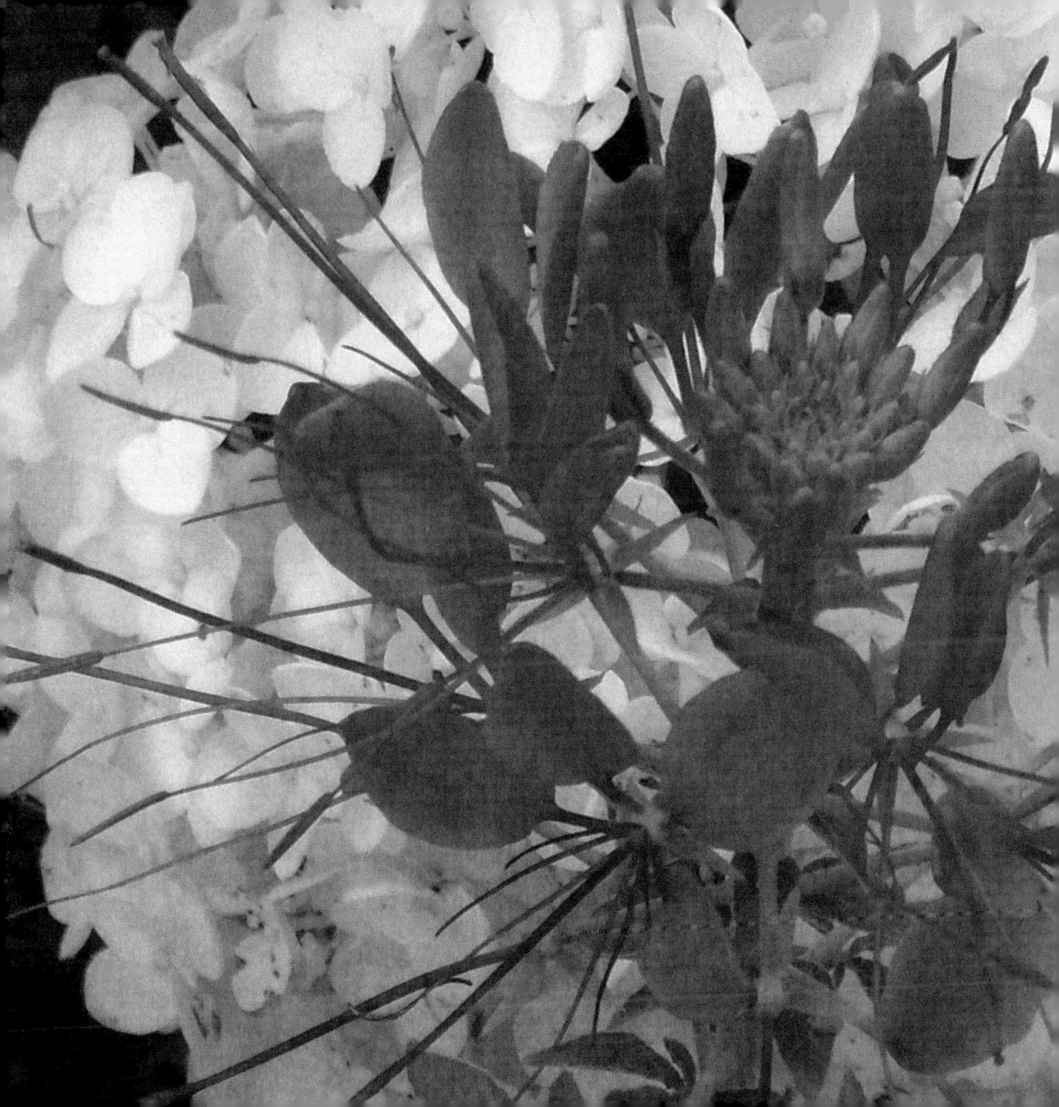

A Fishing License for My Dad

My dad's birthday and the opening of fishing season happen fairly close together, and as a kid, I often bought a fishing license for him as his birthday gift. It was only a few dollars, and he would have bought himself one anyway, but the return on those simple gifts has been enormous. For several of those years, my dad took my brother and me out on an early summer fishing trip to northern Manitoba. On each occasion, the trip was contingent on us getting the spring farm work completed by the scheduled departure date. I learned to plan, organize, motivate those I was working with, avoid distractions, and generally think like a business manager at a very young age in order to hold up my end of the agreement.

And the trips themselves helped me to develop a sense of adventure and exploration. I learned to take calculated risks and gained a greater appreciation for the environment, our country, and the wonder of God's creation. We learned to read maps, and to this day I love maps and any visual representation of information. We learned to seek out remote lakes, and to this day I travel to faraway wilderness locations to experience the land as untouched by man's hand as still exists. We learned to cook, and to this day I love the creative process of turning simple ingredients into gourmet dishes. I learned so many important lessons thanks to my dad, and all of it came from purchasing a few fishing licenses.

**Live a life of adventure and exploration.
When and where do you feel closest to nature?**

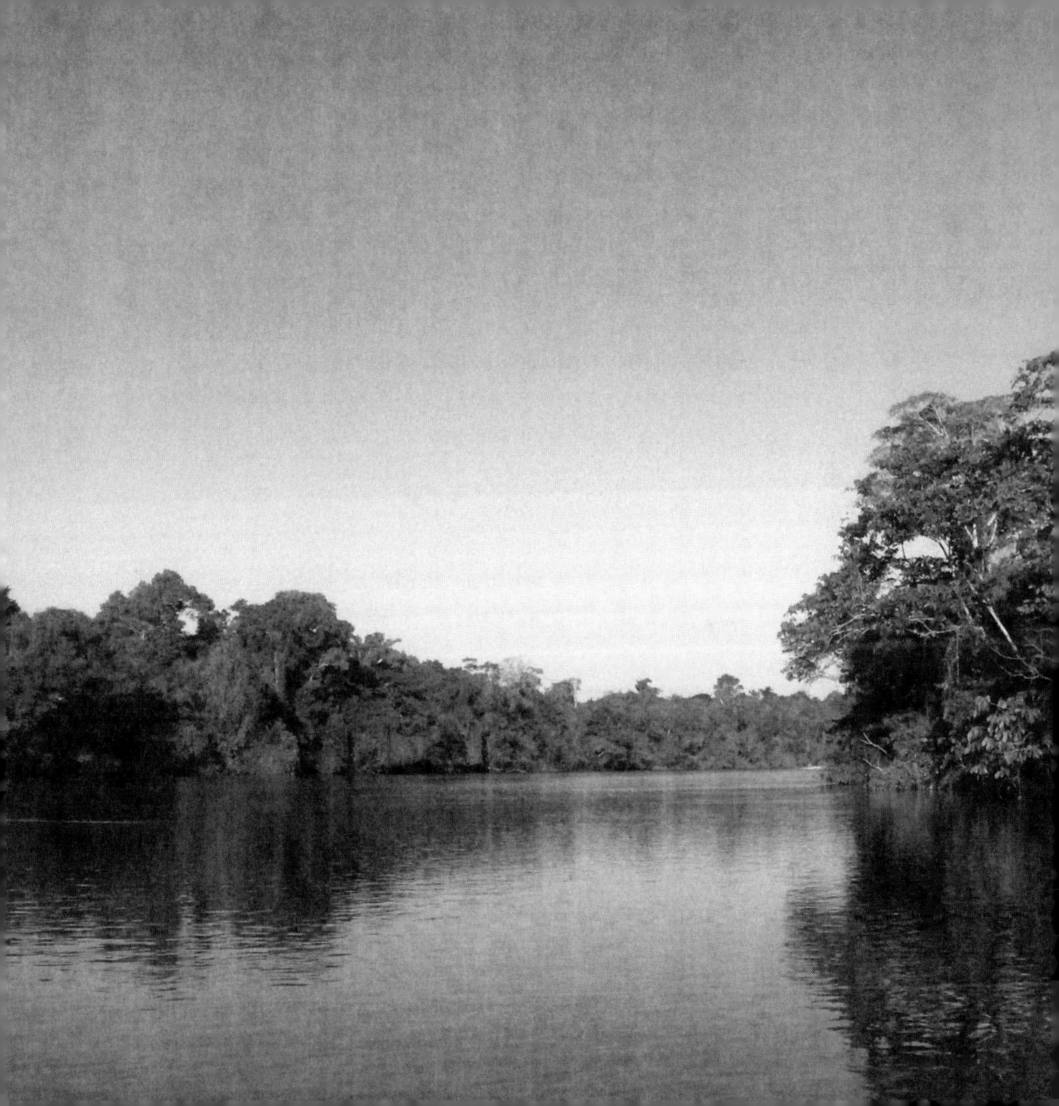

A Tip to a Waitress on Christmas Morning

I was on my way home early on a Christmas morning after visiting my aunt up north about twenty years ago and decided to stop at a restaurant for breakfast. I asked the waitress why she was working so early on Christmas morning. She said she had two small children at home to support. As I had my pancake breakfast, I wrote an encouraging note on a napkin to her, folded it, and put a $20 bill as a tip inside. Boy, did it feel good to be able to do that. Somehow I felt it would brighten her day!

Share the holiday spirit.
Why did you give the biggest tip you have ever given?

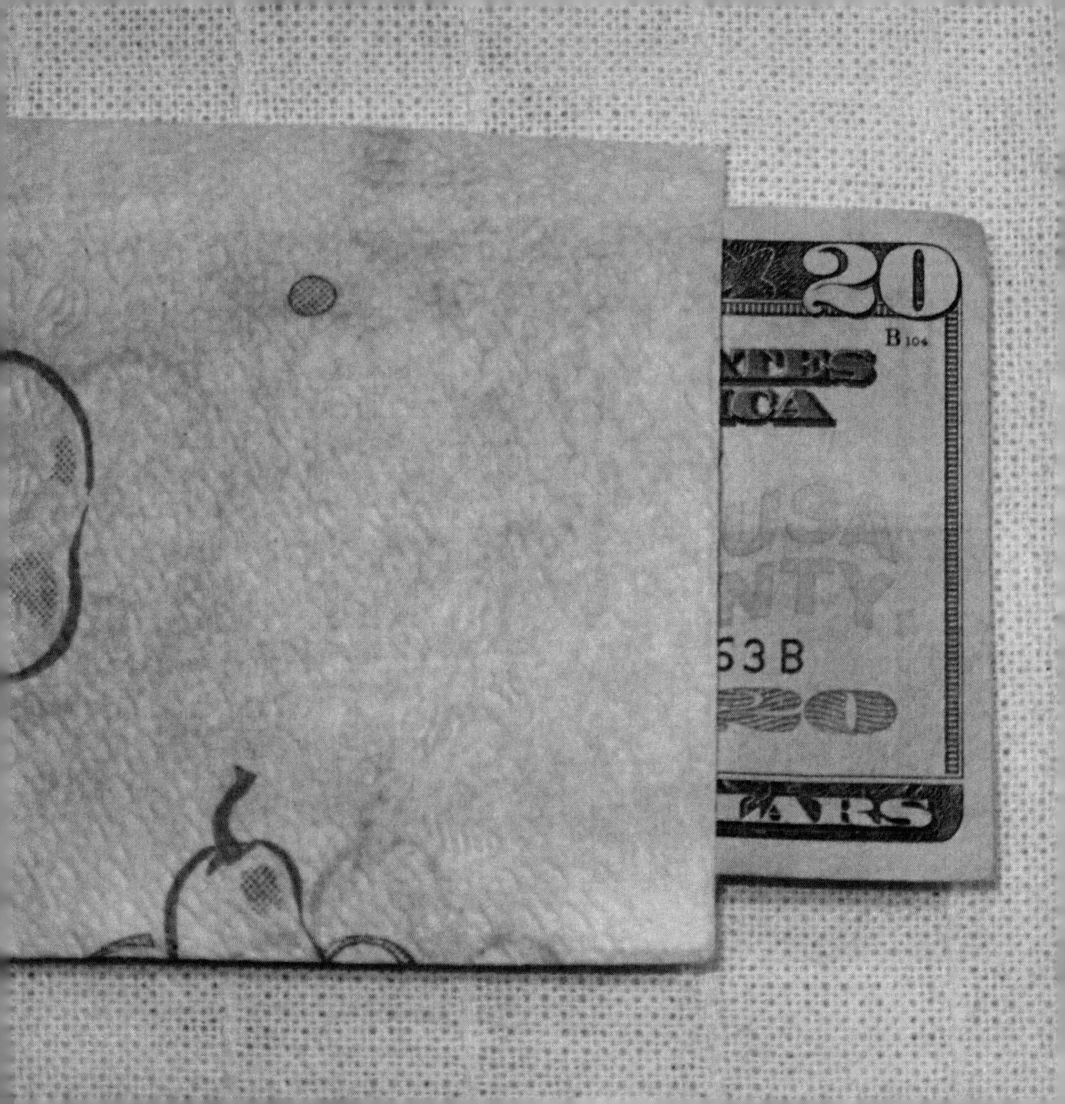
20
B104
63B

A Lottery Ticket

Over twenty years ago, my daughter was involved in a bad car accident and ended up in intensive care. An extremely concerned minister that lived in the neighborhood was very helpful to us, even though he belonged to a different church. He came over several times to make sure my daughter was okay. Fortunately, our daughter recovered all right.

Soon afterward, we bought a lottery ticket and won a nice sum of money. We took our grandkids out for a nice dinner then decided to drive up north where the minister and his wife were building a cabin with what they called their "dream deck." My husband and I wrote a note to them and gave half of the lottery earnings to go toward the deck. We left the envelope for them to open after we left. What a great feeling it was to be able to share our blessings with them!

The world belongs to the givers.
Why is it important to share our blessings with others?

A Ticket to Visit the Nature Center

I bought a ticket to visit a nature center in Florida. While there, I felt part of the planet earth. I felt connected to nature because we are all a part of nature and nature can be part of us while there. I felt happy; I was full of joy and above all at peace with myself when I was there. People should take more time out of their busy lives to be part of nature and enjoy the beauty that is all around them. I am now a regular visitor at our local nature center. When one looks at all the marvel of creation, one can see so much beauty everywhere. The amazing thing is that no two things in nature are the same. There is so much diversity everywhere. I can see that our Creator put so many beautiful plants and animals here on earth for us to enjoy.

Nature is beauty, pure and simple.
What do you do to appreciate and preserve nature?

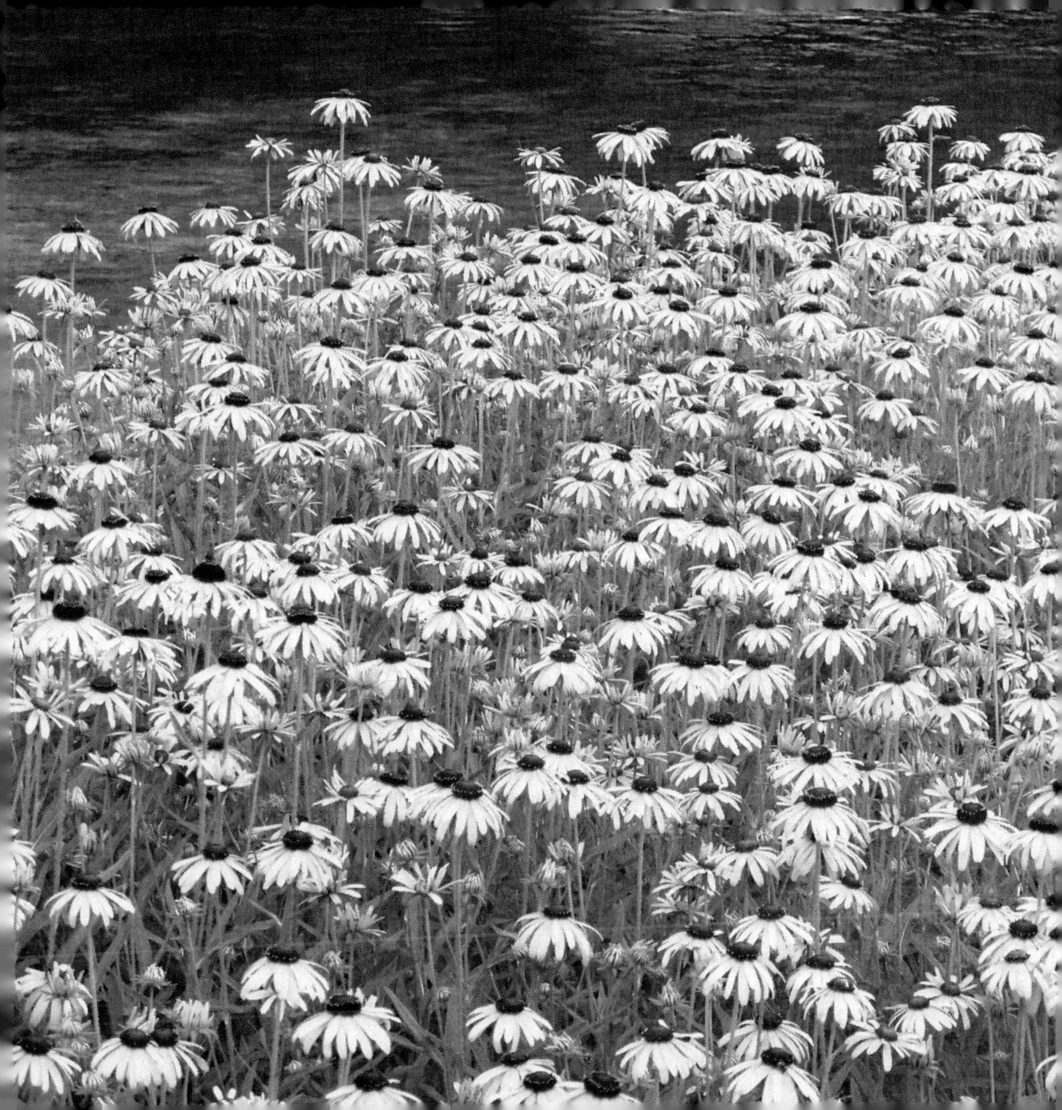

A Hair Cut

An oriental lady came by my hair salon a few months ago. She looked like a homeless person. She needed a haircut badly, so I asked her if she wanted me to cut her hair. She said no and left the salon, but then a few minutes later she came back. I asked her again if I could cut her hair, telling her how beautiful her long hair was. I asked her what nationality she was, and she told me that she was from China. Then I told her that I was from Vietnam.

As I started playing with her hair, she said she did not want a haircut. Realizing she was really stressed, I started giving her a back massage. She then told me how much she liked my salon and asked me how long I had been in that location. I told her five years, and at that point I told her that she needed a hair trim and that I would do it for free. She finally agreed, so I took the time to give her the haircut she needed. She started talking and told me she was a doctor in psychology. She had been in the area for a while and could not find a job, which had led her to be broke and stressed out.

When I was done cutting her hair, she looked like a princess. I told her she was beautiful. She left the store as a changed person. I felt very happy to help her. She came back two weeks later, bringing other people with her. Her demeanor had changed, and she looked so much better. I have given many free haircuts over the years, but this one touched me the most. God has given me so many blessings, so I have to bless others. Many people come here heavy and leave light. I give them hope, faith, and above all love.

Giving from the heart is the purest form of giving.
How do you make best use of your talents to comfort others?

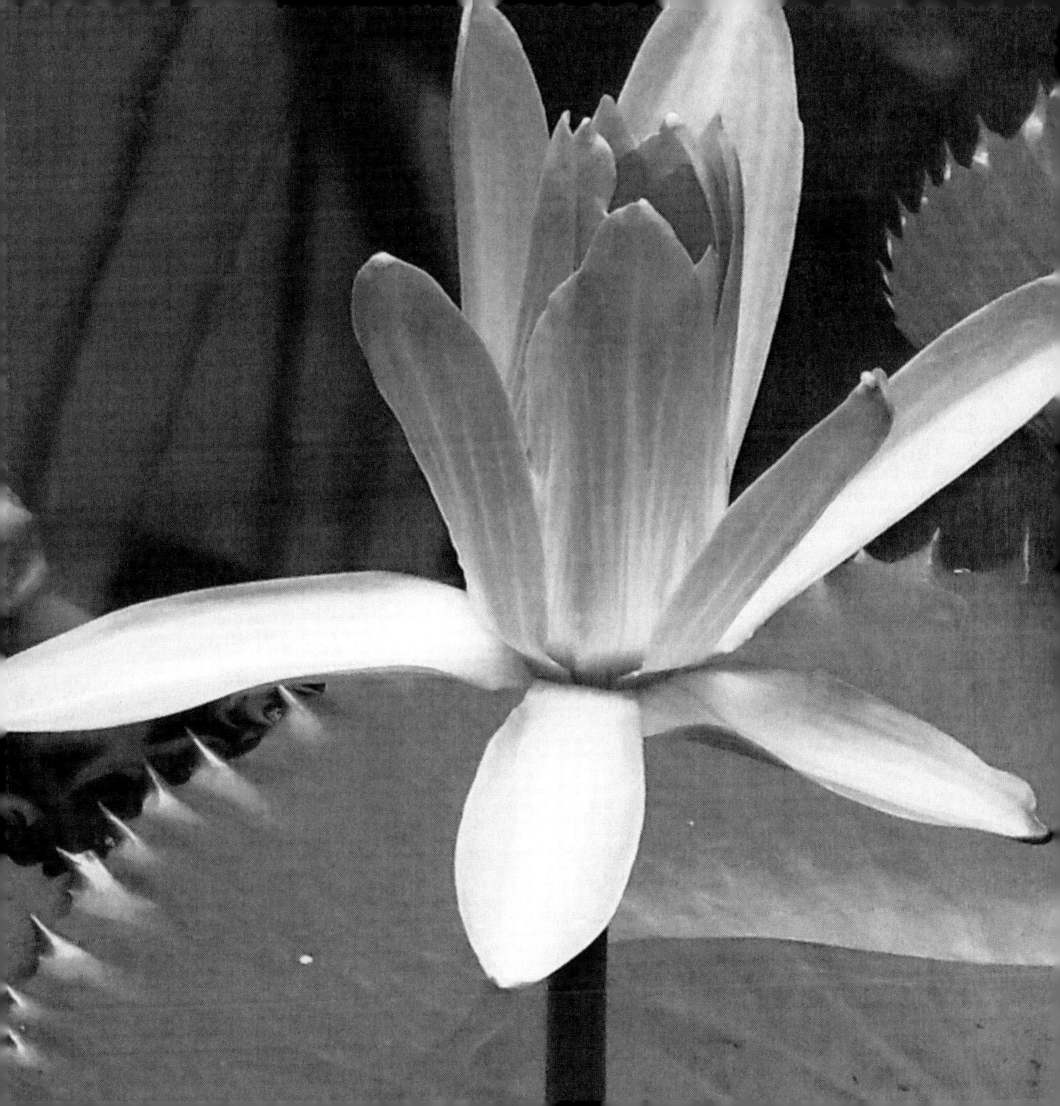

A Pack of Gum

When I was eighteen years old and a freshman at Kalamazoo College, a girl came to me and asked if I was chewing gum. I said yes. However, I did not have any gum with me, so I went to my dorm room and got a stick of gum for her. We were friends for three years before we started dating. Today, she is my wife of eleven years. We have three beautiful children. Little did I know that a walk back to my room to get a stick of gum was going to be the beginning of the most important relationship of my life. Maybe we were going to meet in the small college anyway and become friends. We often talk about how we met as freshman. I see marriage as a commitment forever. It takes a lot of work to make a marriage work, but it's worth it.

**Love is in beauty, and beauty is where love is found.
How did you go about choosing the person you married?**

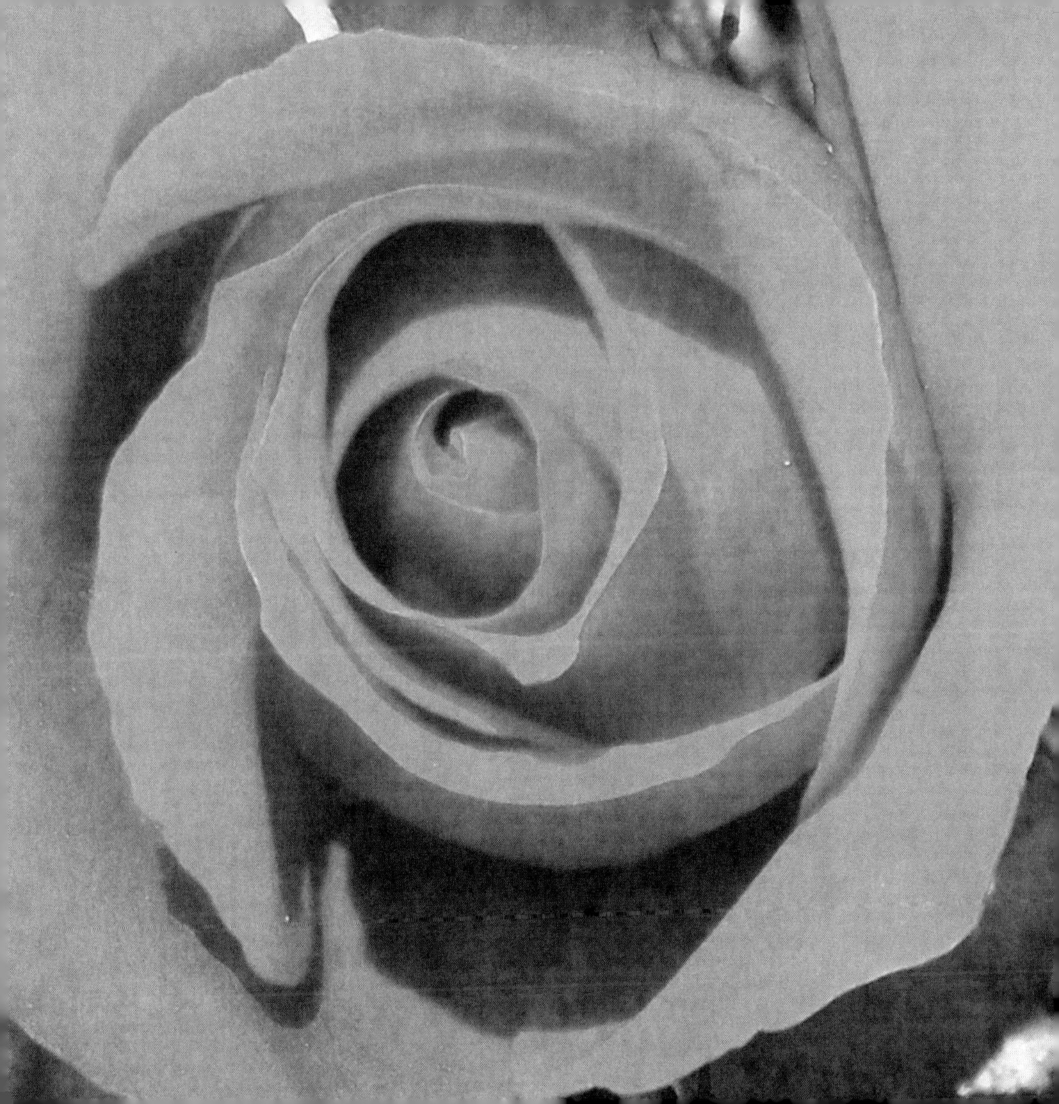

An Adopted Daughter

My wife and I adopted a baby girl forty-one years ago for a total cost of $12. When I reflect upon this now, it definitely was the best value we got for a small amount of money. She was only nine days old when we adopted her. Adopting was a lot easier back in those days. She brought greater fulfillment into our lives than we could have even realized. We became a complete family since we had already adopted a son one and a half years earlier. She made us laugh all the time. She helped me to become a stronger man and a protective father. She grew up to become a responsible, beautiful person and gave birth to two lovely grandchildren. Our grandson was born with near blindness due to an incurable disease. He has been nothing but a blessing in our lives. We have had so many precious moments with our grandchildren. We paid a very small price for the high reward of adopting our daughter. I highly recommend adoption for those who would like to give a child a loving home.

**A united family grows and stays together.
What would you be willing to sacrifice
to give a child a better future?**

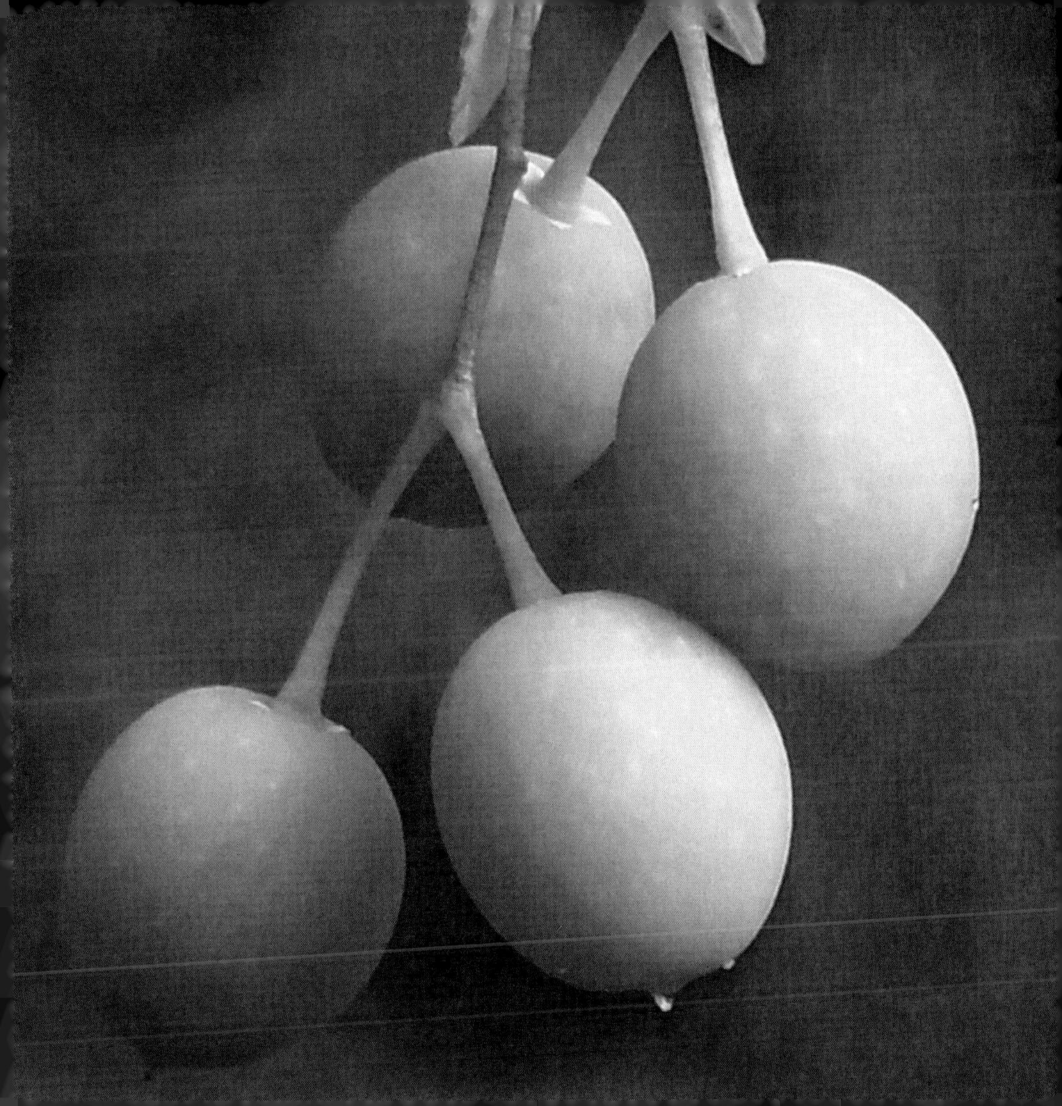

STORIES OF LEGACY

An Italian-American Club Membership

After finishing college, I spent a small sum of money on a membership into the Italian-American Club. The membership at the club allowed me the chance to associate with several influential individuals. The positive association that I had with the other members led me to a great job that quadrupled my income. The new job and the new association with others allowed me to start a career in the field of mechanical engineering, which was the focus of my studies. The interesting part of this story is that I have no Italian heritage whatsoever!

Success is the freedom to be who you are.
What are the most important associations in your life?

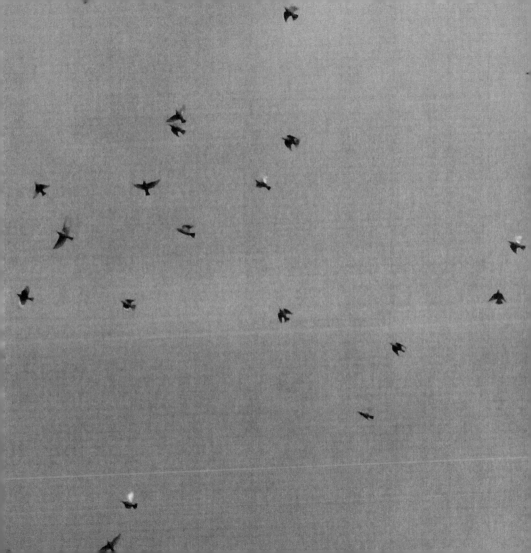

The *Ramona* Book Series

The best investment I have ever made was in a little book series called *Ramona* by Beverly Cleary. The book expanded my imagination, and I started to develop the powerful habit of reading. I started sharing with others the value of reading great books. Now a book is my favorite gift to give others. That is also why I became a librarian. Books have a calming effect on me. I love being around books!

Powerful words affirm and inspire us.
What is the book that has most impacted your life?

LEADERSHIP GOLD

... BECOMING A PERSON OF INFLUENCE

LIFE IS TREMENDOUS — JONES

IT MATTERS MOST — *The Power of Living Your Values* — Hyrum W.

SIMON SAYS — CHUCK GOETSCHEL

IN A PIT WITH A LION ON A SNOWY DAY — MARK BAT...

RETURN OF THE PRODIGAL SON — HENRI J. M. N...

BITS OF HIGHLY EFFECTIVE PEOPLE

THERE'S NO SUCH THING AS "BUSINESS" ETHICS — JO... MAX...

A Gallon of Gas

Years ago I went to the gas station to buy gas for my lawnmower. When I was returning home to cut the grass, I passed by someone that was stranded on the side of the road. I stopped to help this fellow who needed gas by giving him my gallon can full of gas. He thanked me, and we each went our separate ways. I never saw that person again. It felt great to inconvenience myself to help someone else in need. I paid it forward because I know that individual someday will likely do something similar to help someone else, perhaps even to another stranger!

Paying forward pays backward.
How do you feel after helping someone in need?

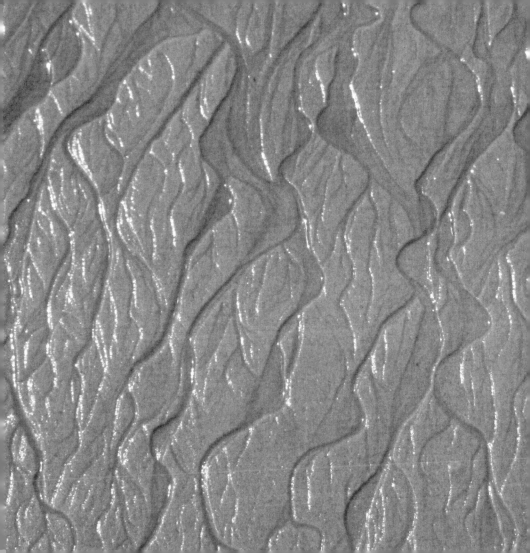

Donations for Nieces and Nephews

The best small investment I have ever made was the small donation I made for my nieces and nephews from a catalog many years ago. Instead of giving children money, I helped them to shop from a catalog and then donate things as presents to others. I felt it was very important to teach them about giving to less fortunate children during the holidays. It felt great to teach them that giving to others is better than receiving!

We all play a role in educating younger generations.
What are you doing to help young people
learn the power of giving?

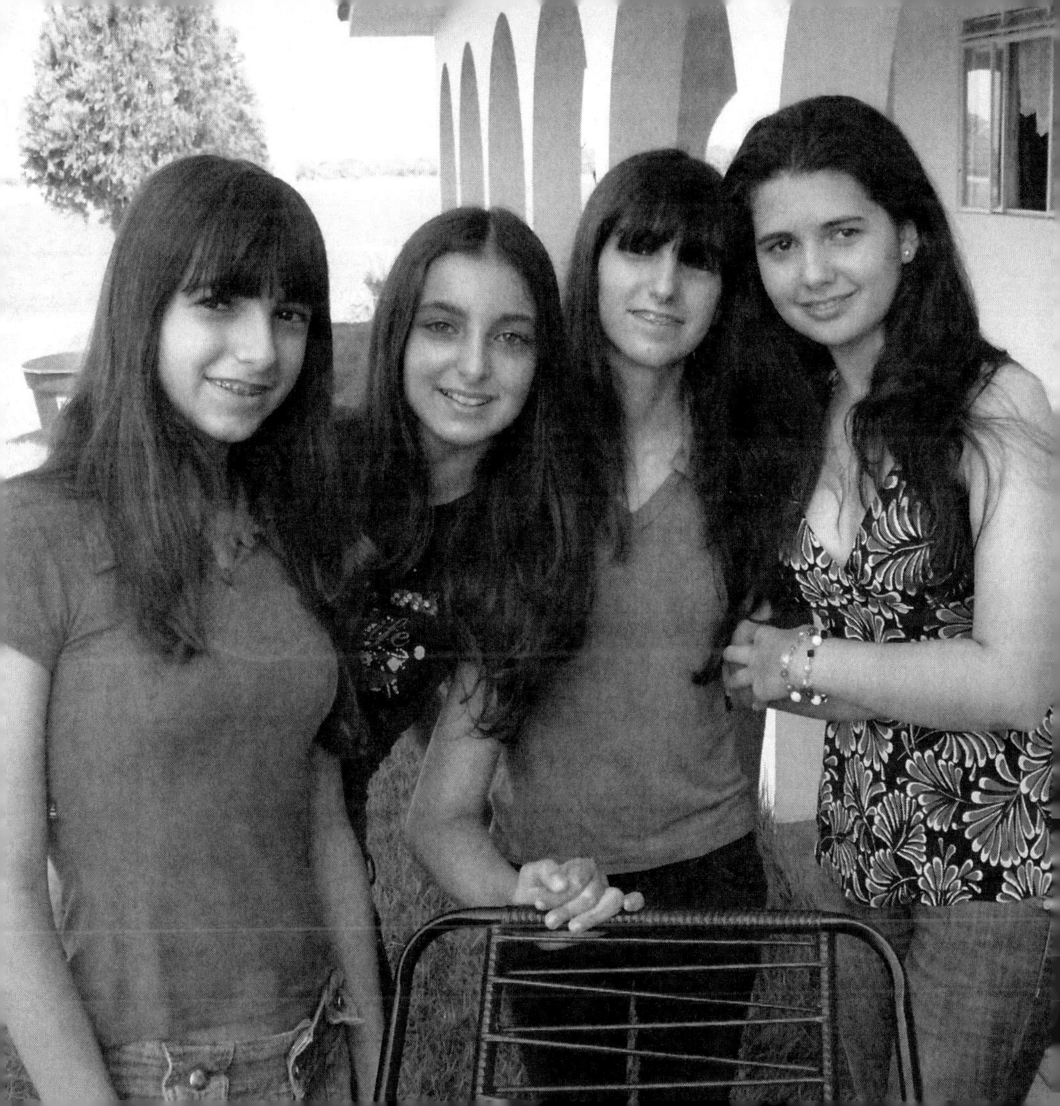

Poster Supplies

When I was in high school, I was part of the pro-life group at school. One year we made some posters to put up around the school to spread the pro-life message. I spent about $10 on supplies to make my poster, which said, "Abortion: it doesn't make you un-pregnant; it makes you the mother of a dead baby." This phrase may sound harsh, but as it turned out, it was just the right one to use. There was a girl at our school who was pregnant and intending to have an abortion. She sought out our teacher to tell him that the sign caused her to change her mind. She decided to give life to her baby boy. After this experience, I am now a very outspoken pro-life advocate. I hope to help change our society's mind about abortion.

The positive ripple effect of a human life lasts forever.
What is the value of a human life?

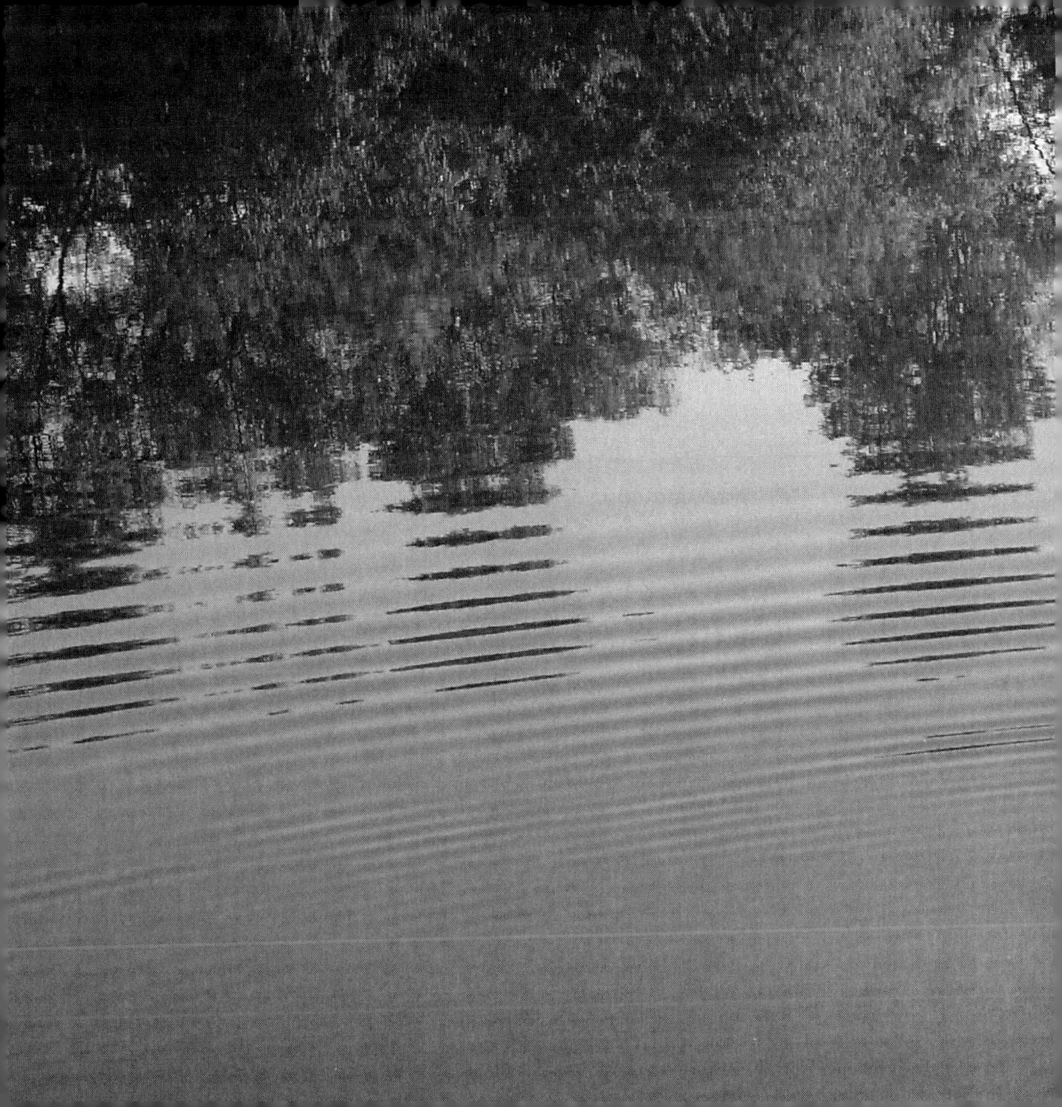

A Ride Home

Years ago a stranger came up to me and asked to borrow $10. This person was living in a tent at a campground and needed money to get home. My first thought was, *This fellow is going to use the money to buy something like alcohol or cigarettes.* Years later, I was completely surprised when the individual came to pay the money back to me. He had turned his life around and insisted on paying me double. He had since held a job and pursued and succeeded in securing a veteran's pension. The interesting thing is that now he spends a significant portion of his income on helping other people. He came back to see me again just a few days ago. What a great investment that $10 turned out to be! It is a great feeling to be surprised by something like this. My faith in people has increased because of this experience! We ought to have faith and respect everyone, but trust is earned, as this experience taught me.

Faith comes from having strong belief.
How are you a blessing to others?

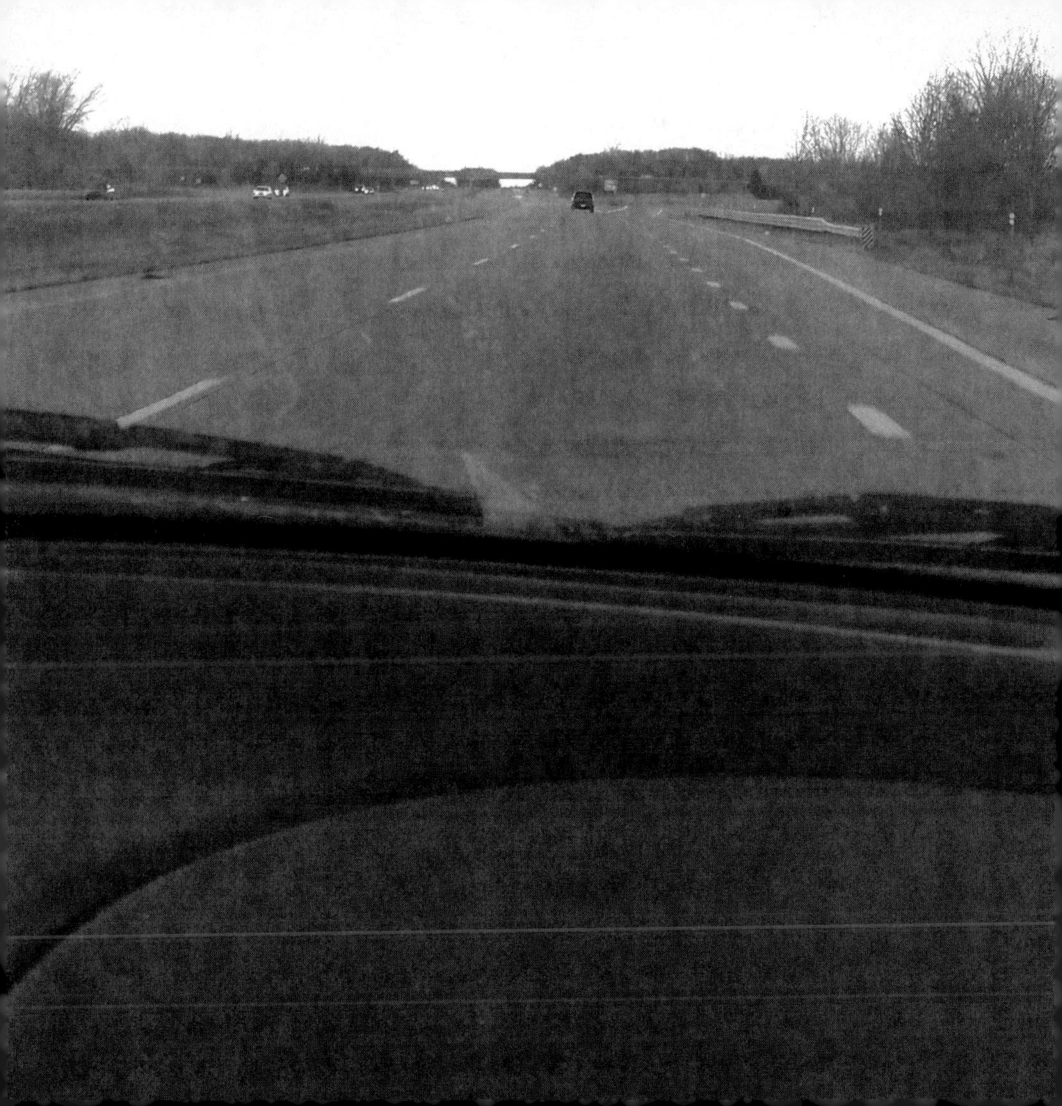

A Mass for My Parents' Souls

A few years ago I spent $10 to have a Mass said for the repose of my parents' souls. I did it in gratitude for them giving me a healthy physical and spiritual life. My parents gave me a great education and a strong Catholic faith. They influenced who I became and what I did with my life. The biggest blessing has been that I now know that I have the key to my salvation and that we will be together for eternity!

Eternity is a long time to be wrong.
What were the top twenty-five lessons that
you learned from your parents?

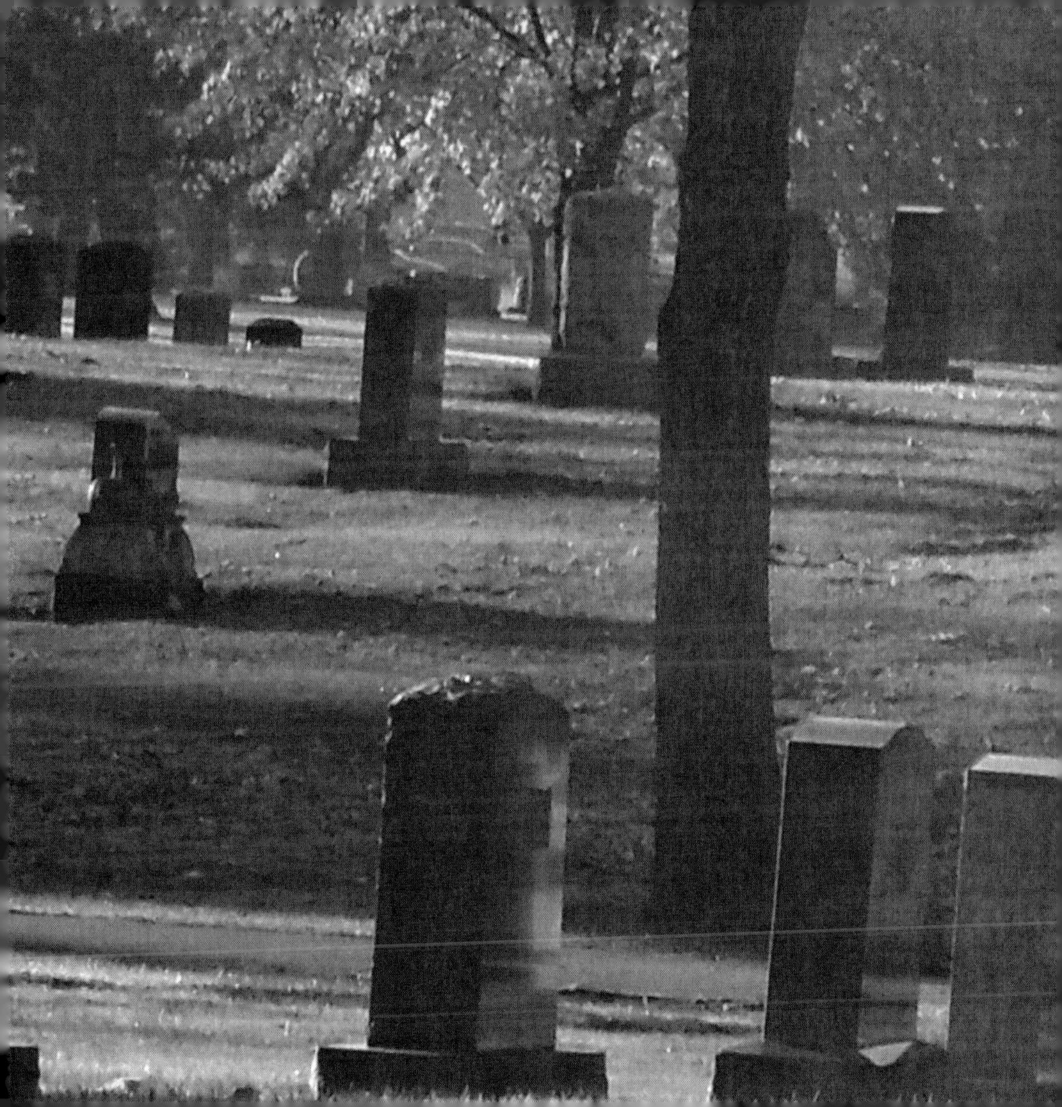

A Psychological Study

Years ago I bought a paperback book and read about the "Marshmallow Experiment." I followed up and got detailed information about the experiment. I was so intrigued that I decided to repeat the experiment in another country (Colombia) and decided to write my own book about the concept: *Don't Eat the Marshmallow...Yet!* I wrote the book, and the rest is history! I sold two million copies of the book and made a small fortune!

Only applied knowledge is power.
How do you apply what you learn from reading great books?

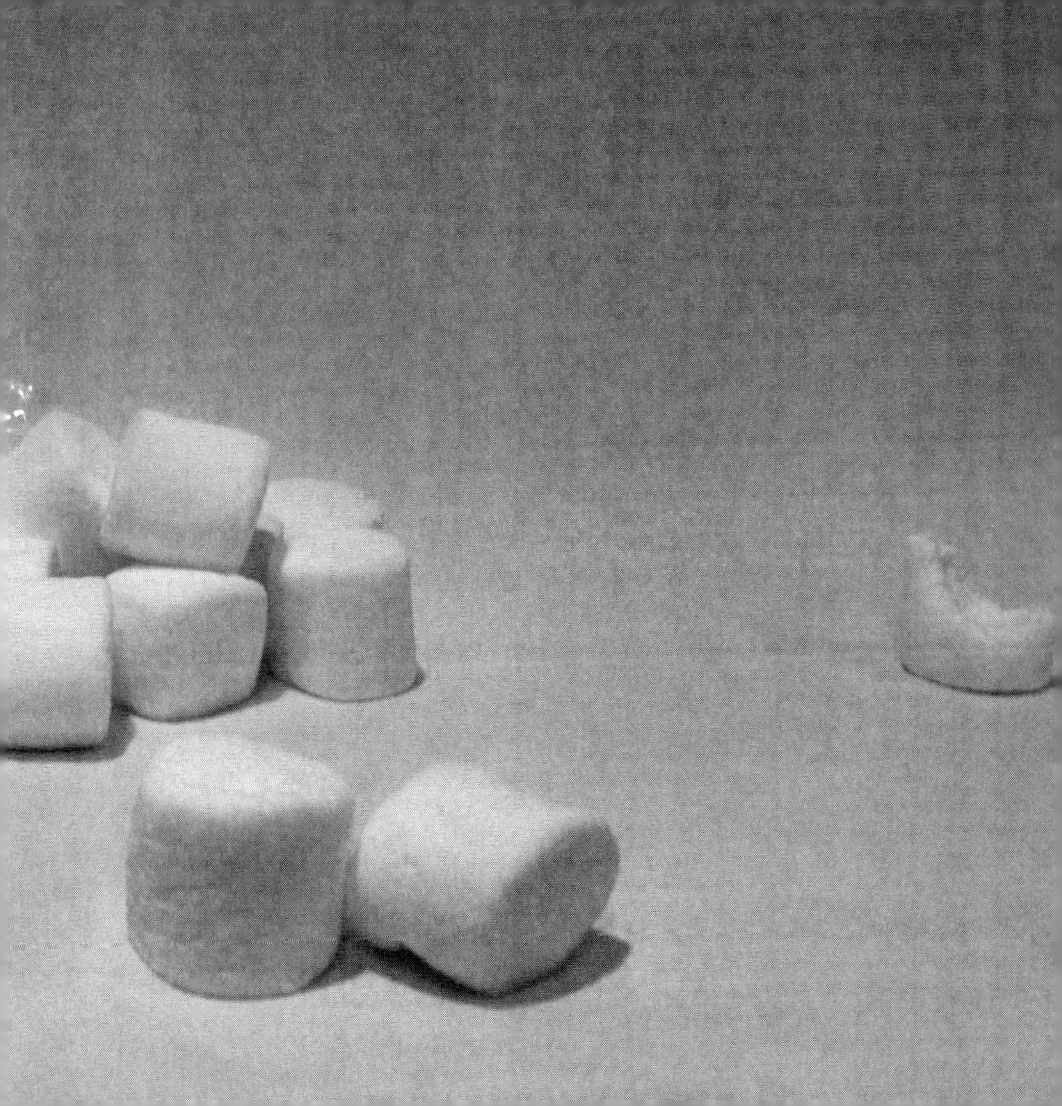

A Christmas Gift for My Mother

The best $10 I spent was on a Christmas gift for my mom and dad about ten years ago. We were short on money, so I decided to make gifts for my parents that year. My mother had saved one of her childhood dolls all these years, but it was falling apart due to dry rot. It also had no clothing and had always been stored in her wedding dress box. A few years earlier, my parents moved to Europe, and she entrusted her doll's care to me. I took the doll to a doll repair shop and had the body restrung, but she was still without clothing.

At home, I had many doll patterns and fabric from making doll clothes for my daughter. I decided to make a dress, apron, and bloomers, making her look similar to how she must have been decades earlier. I wrapped her in tissue paper, put her in a gift box, and placed her under the tree for Mom.

For Dad, I wanted to let him know how much I appreciated his love and support through the years. I began writing down child-hood memories of my father. Once I'd completed it, I printed it in calligraphy and framed it. I called it, "50 Fondest Memories of My Dad." This was then wrapped and placed under the tree.

On Christmas Eve, we had our traditional gift exchange. I wasn't really sure what Mom and Dad would think about their gifts and started to feel guilty about not spending much on them. Mom went first, opening the box and expecting a store-bought gift. When she opened the tissue paper, tears filled her eyes as she said, "Oh my gosh. I got this doll for Christmas over forty years ago, and here she is, as beautiful as she was then." She was truly surprised.

Then Dad opened his gift. My father is a man of few words, and after he read his gift, he too had tears in his eyes. I followed by saying how much I loved them both and wanted to give them a gift from my heart that year. Today, Dad's gift is proudly displayed on his home office wall, and Mom's doll has the place of honor in the center of her curio cabinet.

**The holiday season is for giving and receiving.
What was the best Christmas gift you have ever given?**

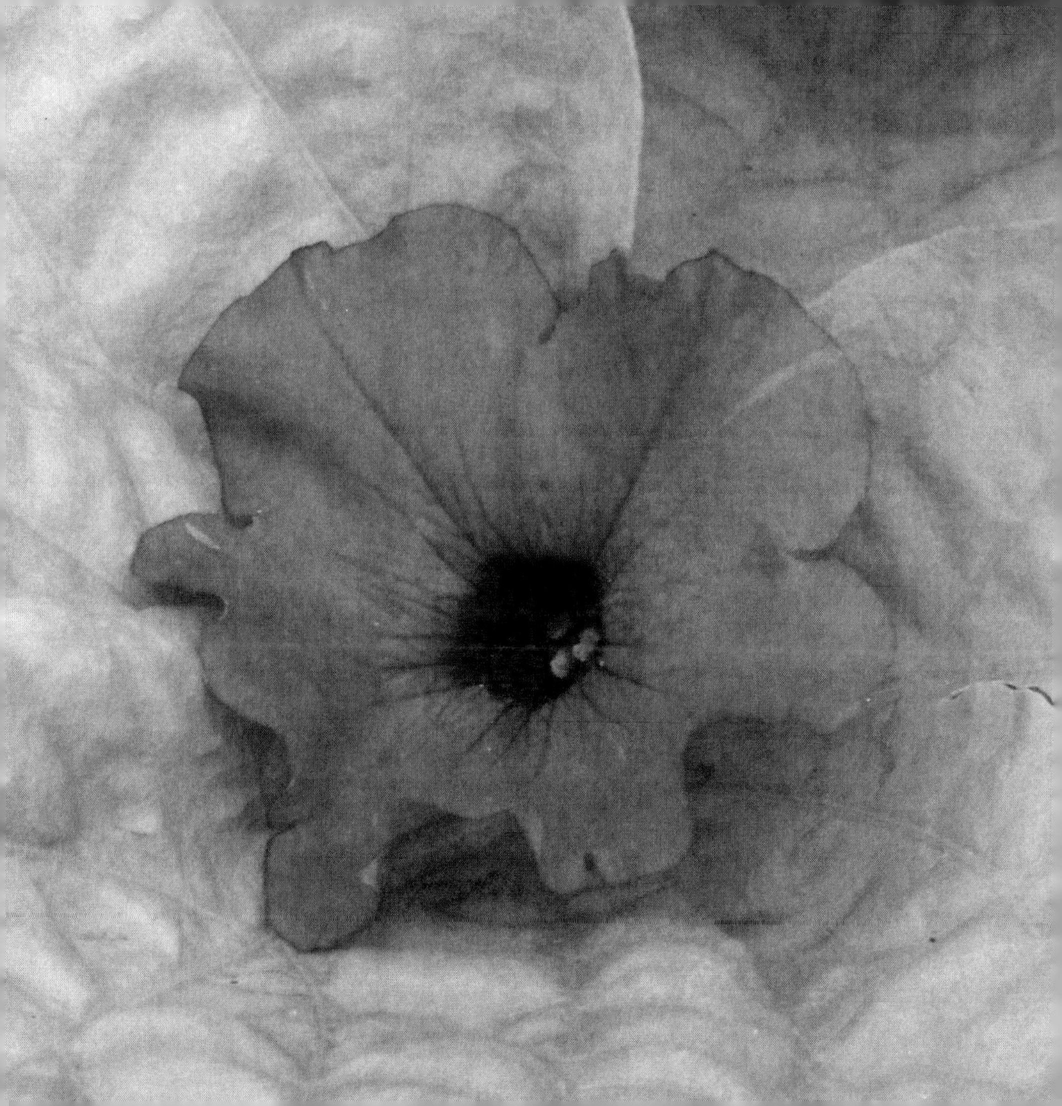

A Drink for a Marine

I am in awe of our service men and women. I never served and will regret it all of my life. While in my seat for a flight to Las Vegas during boarding, two marines went by and took their seats a few rows in back of mine. When a flight attendant came past for the final check before takeoff, I handed her a twenty and asked that those marines got what they wanted to drink when service became available. She said she would do what she could. A few moments later, she came back and said she could do better than that as she gave me back my twenty. The captain came on over the PA system and requested that the marines come forward to be seated in first class. The entire plane cheered as they made their way forward. The marines were the ones then to send me back a drink!

In altitude, we find gratitude.
What is the best thing you have done for
a member of our armed forces?

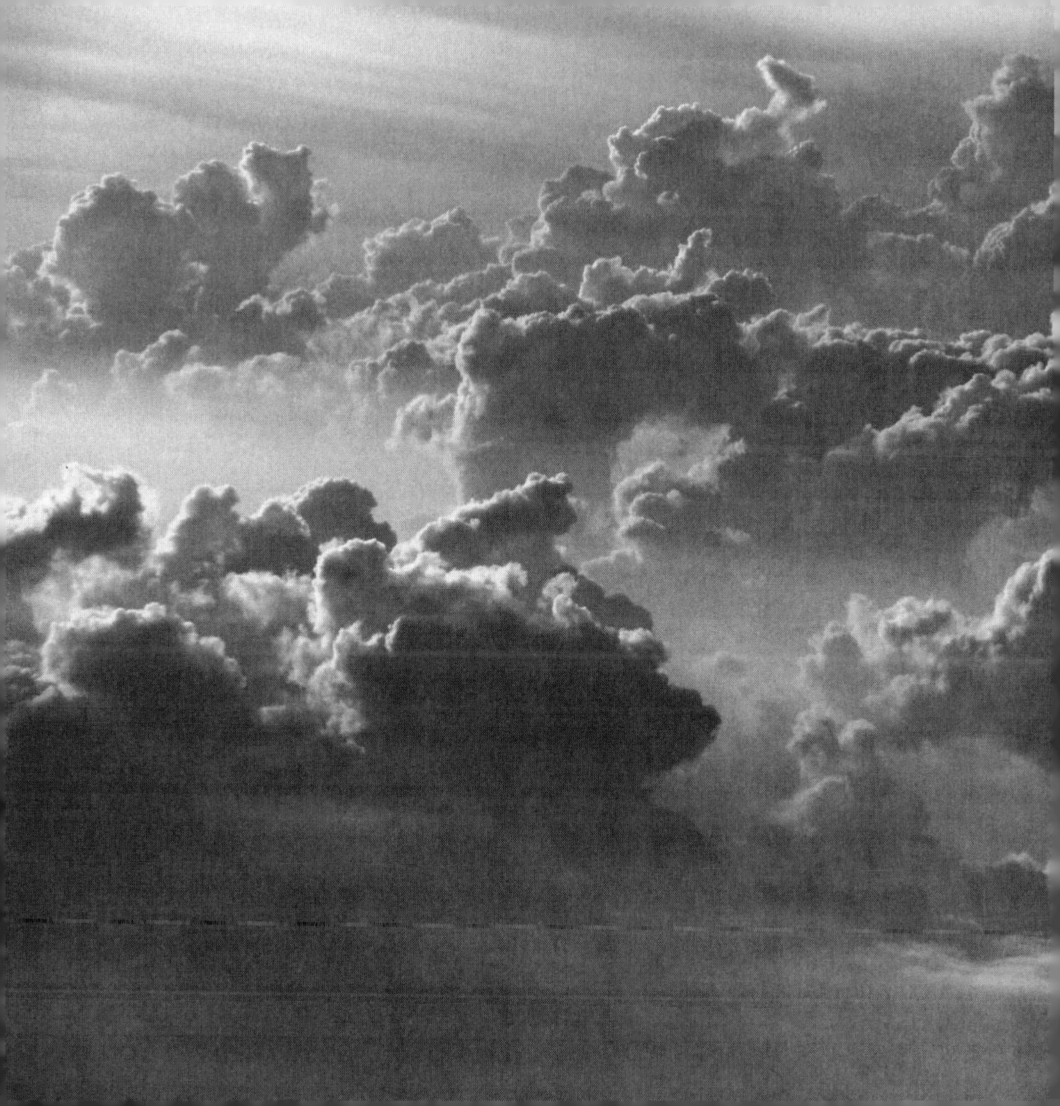

A Token of Appreciation
for a Soldier

In 2006, at a local restaurant, there was a gentleman in his mid-twenties wearing a US military uniform. A thought came to my mind that someone ought to pay for his lunch! I asked the waitress if she would add his lunch bill to mine so the gentleman's lunch could be paid without him knowing who paid. She said okay. She walked over to his table to serve him more iced tea. She told him someone had already taken care of his bill in appreciation for his service to the country. I could see from the corner of my left eye as they were talking. At first he looked somewhat surprised and then looked around with a soft, big smile on his young face. A feeling of gratitude ran through my spine as I watched his smiling face from the adjacent room.

The best gratitude is found when least expected.
How do you demonstrate gratitude for those
who preserve our precious freedom?

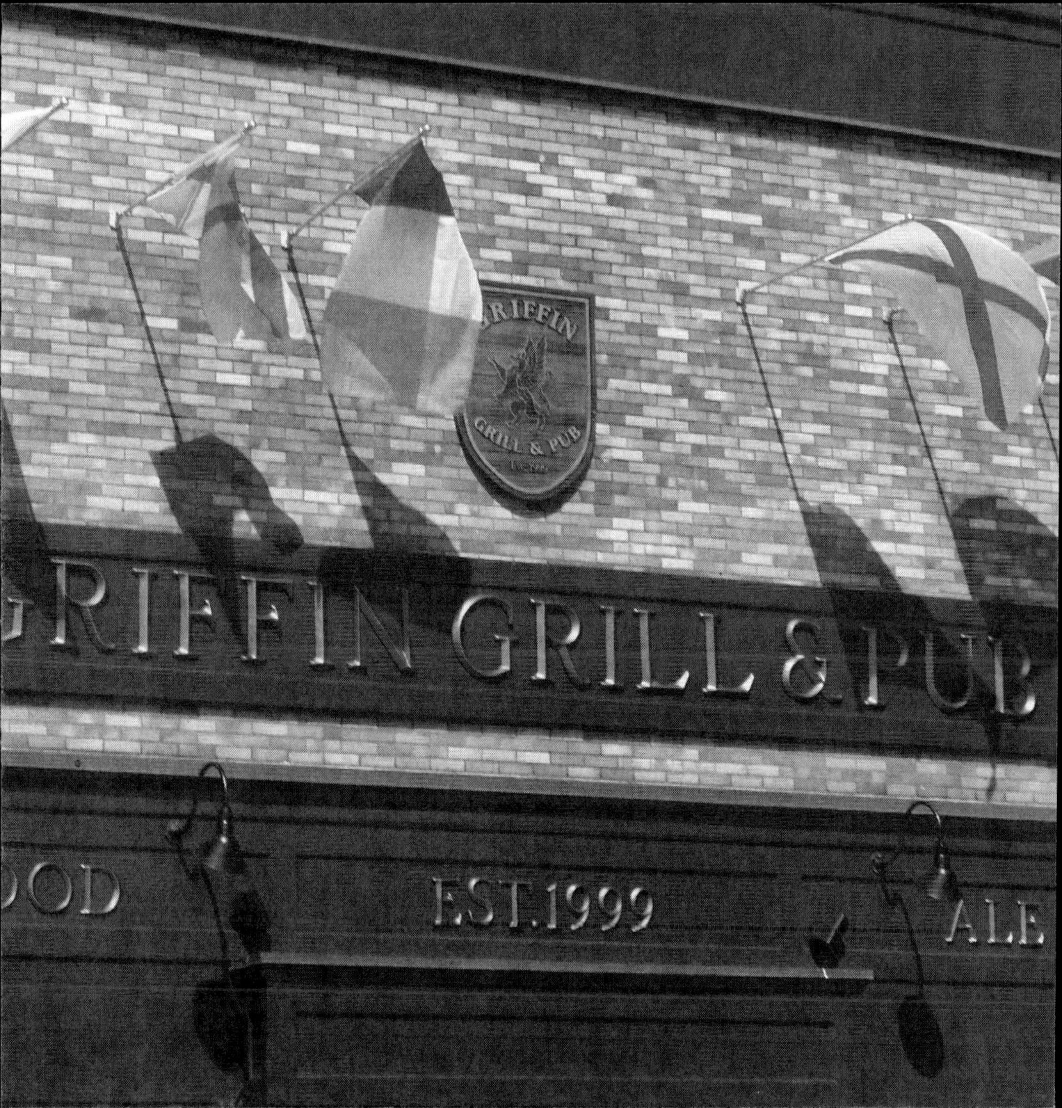
GRIFFIN GRILL & PUB
GRILL & PUB
GRIFFIN GRILL & PUB
OOD
EST.1999
ALE

A Friendship Necklace

Three years ago I bought a butterfly necklace at the Binder Park Zoo in Michigan. I love butterflies because they are very pretty. Butterflies remind me of grace, beauty, freedom, and friendship. Even though I loved the necklace, I handed it to my best friend so she could wear it during her confirmation at her church. She liked the necklace a lot. I feel like I shared a part of me with my friend. She would do anything for me no matter what happened to me. She is a true friend, and she will be there for me if I ever need anything or need help going through any hardship in my life. My friend is now planning to pass the necklace on to one of her friends. I feel like we started a tradition to pass the butterfly necklace from friend to friend!

True friends have protected bonds.
What is the most cherished gift you have ever given to a friend?

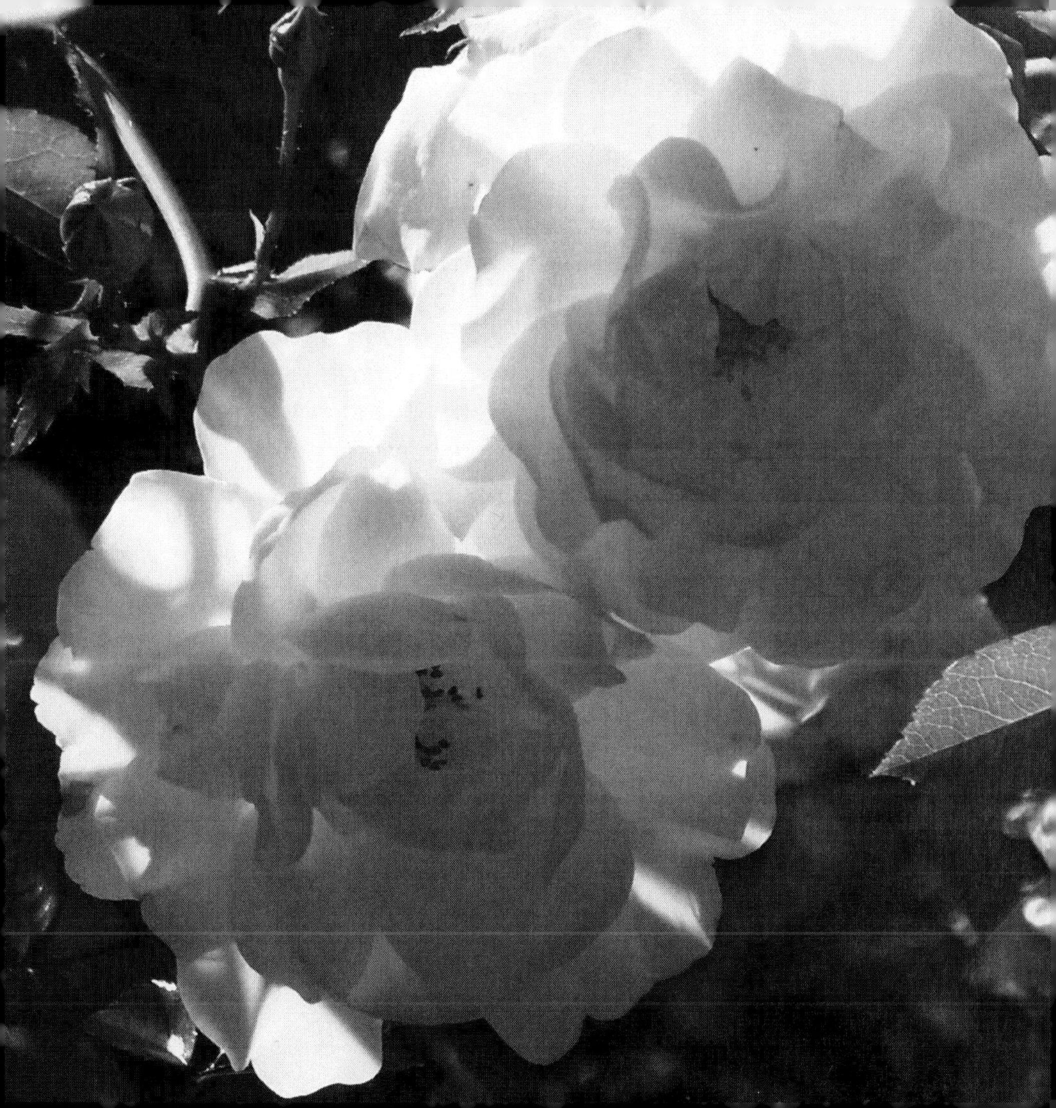

Food and Drinks for Those Less Fortunate Than I

The best small investment I have ever made was to give food and drinks to people who could not afford to buy them on their own. The giving provided me with a positive outlook on my life. I think my café customers started seeing what I was doing, and that gave them a positive outlook in their lives, too. The amazing thing was that the giving turned out to be a big positive for my business as well. The customers gave me loyalty because they saw what I was doing for those in need.

**The seeds of love spread widely.
What feelings come to you after giving
something for others to eat?**

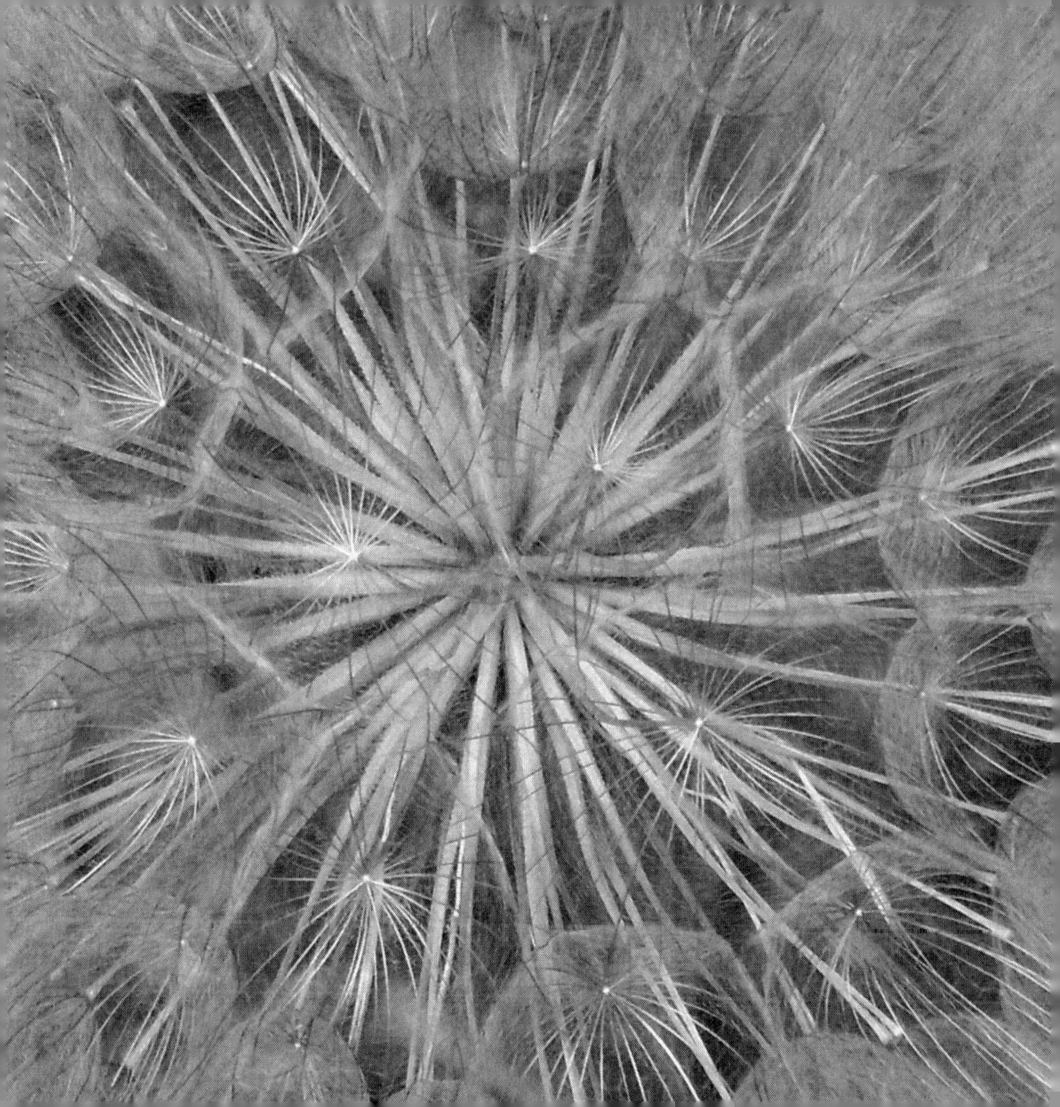

Baked Cookies

I started baking Christmas cookies for my neighbors twenty-eight years ago. I loved going to their houses to give them cookies because they always liked to see me coming during the holidays. Three years ago I told my neighbors that I would no longer be baking cookies for the holidays. To my surprise, the neighbors got together and brought baking ingredients to my front door, and they asked me if I would continue baking cookies. You can guess what happened then. I am still baking cookies for my neighbors, and last year I even baked cookies for my coworkers.

Serving others is the greatest of all callings.
What are your thoughts when making presents
for others during the holidays?

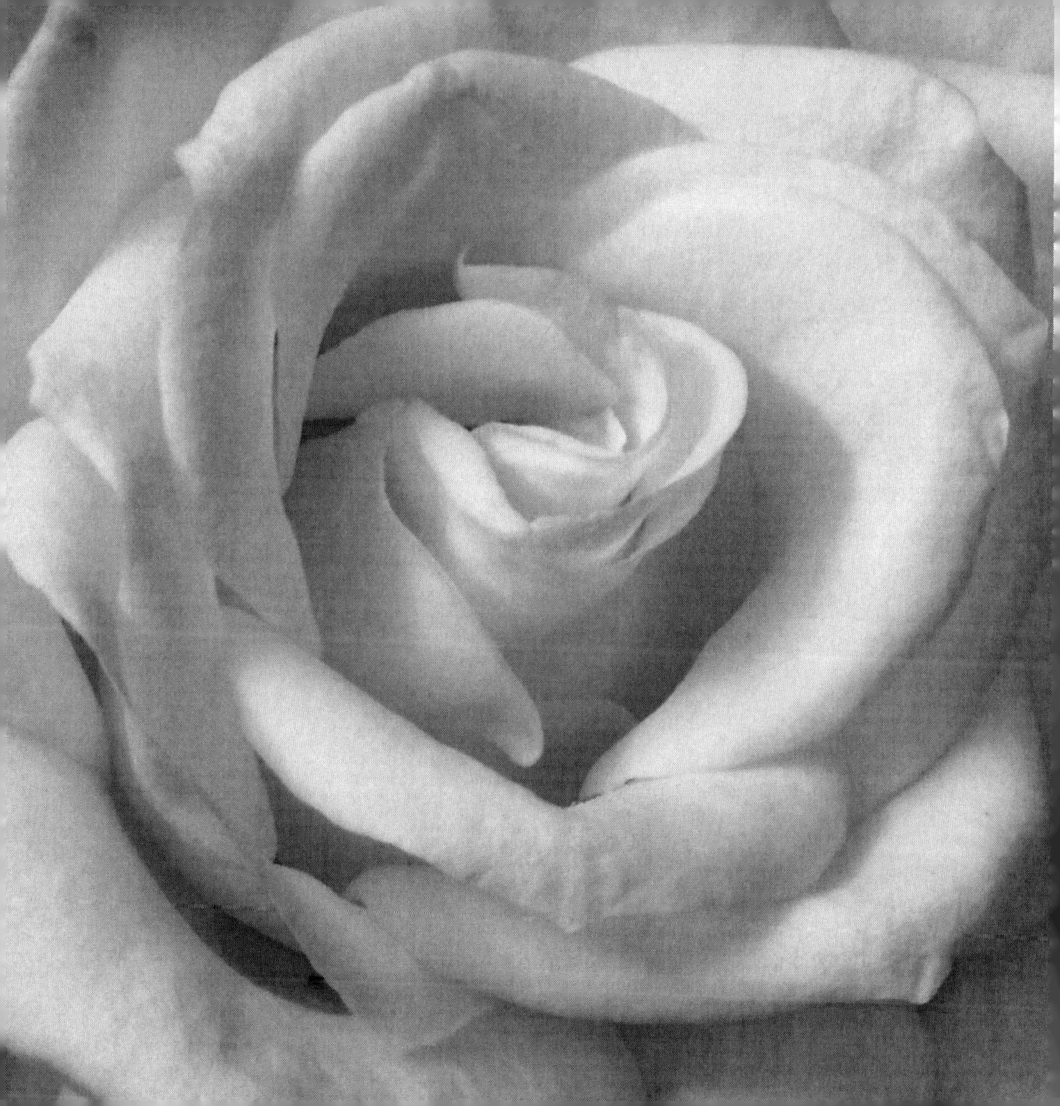

A Kidney Donation to My Cousin

The best investment I have ever made was to pay $10 for gas for someone to give me a ride to a hospital so I could be tested for a kidney donation. It turned out the tests were positive, and I was able to successfully donate one of my kidneys to my cousin in Ohio. I felt it was important to inconvenience myself so he could live. After I donated one of my kidneys, I gained some weight, which is a side effect of the kidney donation procedure. It is totally okay with me though. The thought that I helped my cousin to stay alive is a great feeling that will last forever!

Healthy seeds sustain life.
Would you donate one of your organs to give life to someone?

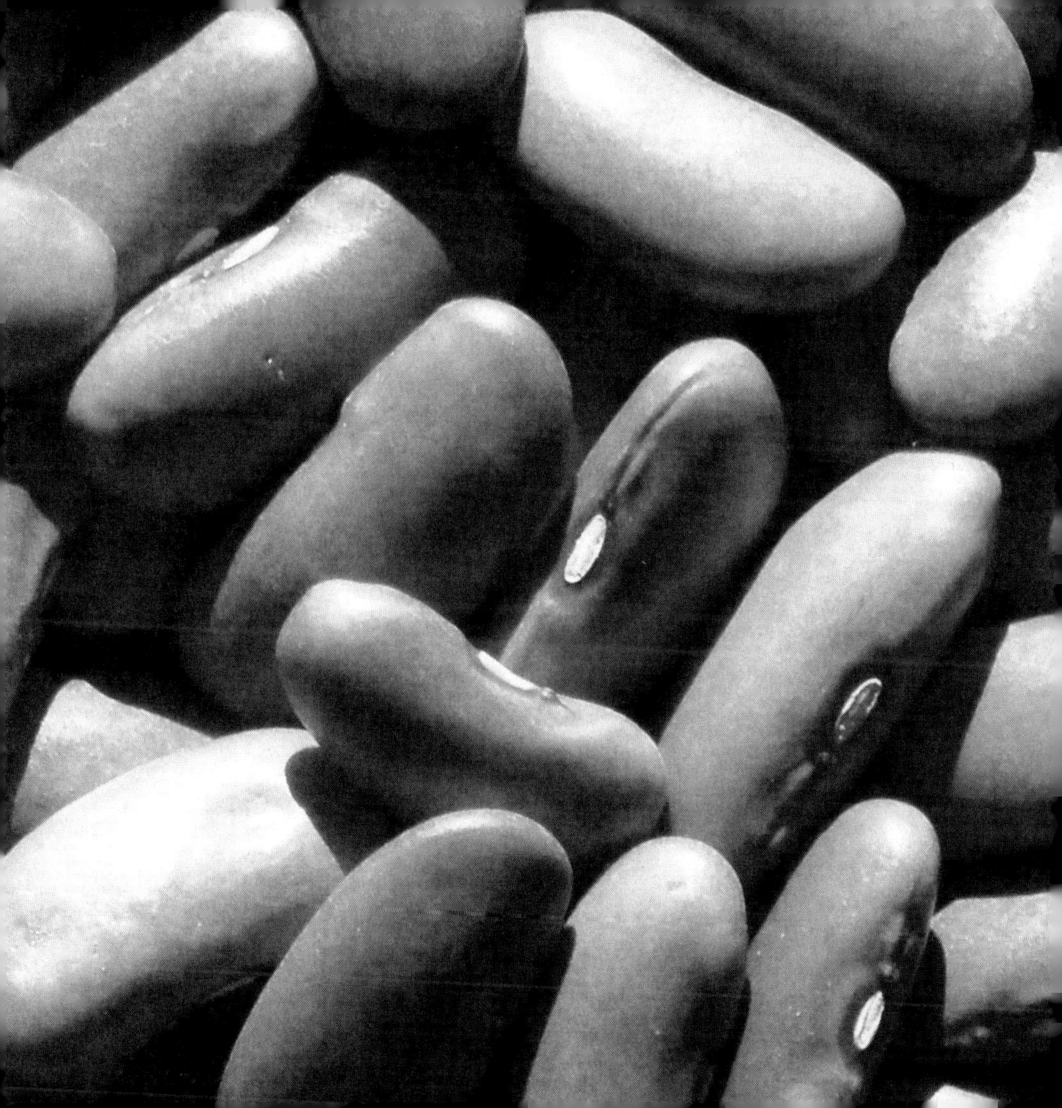

Coffee with My Mother

The best $10 I have ever spent was to have fresh brewed coffee and go for a walk with my eighty-year-old mother. She is a very special woman, as she raised three daughters as a single parent. She has always kept the four of us very close in our friendships. The four of us still talk daily, and that is how we stay so close. I am very happy today as we walk here by the river enjoying our coffee. We treasure the time we spend with each other. We are always learning from her, and she is a great source of wisdom. Now we are trying to convince our mother to move in with one of us as the time is coming for us to take care of her.

**Walking is healthy for the body and the mind.
How do you treasure the time you spend
with your mother or father?**

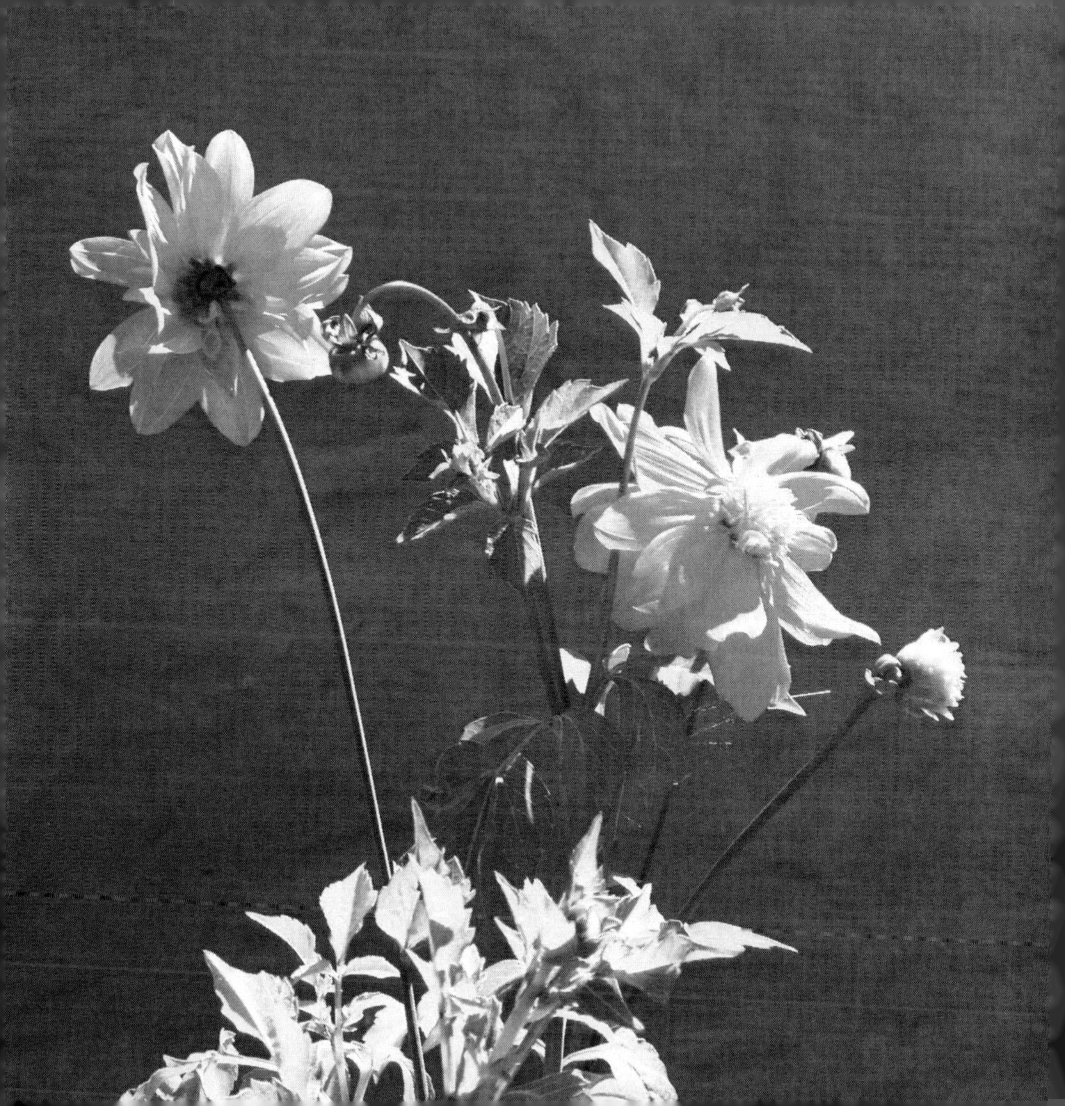

A Book for My Mother

I took care of my mother while she was dying of cancer. At the time, I was bitter because my siblings did not want to help care for her. Now as I look back, I feel it was their loss and not mine. I have now fully forgiven them, and I feel blessed. My mother loved to read books written by Louis L'Amour. L'Amour wrote many novels and short-story collections and called his writing "Frontier Stories." Mother loved to read his books because they ignited her imagination, and she always looked forward to when I would bring her a new book. We really enjoyed the time we spent together during her last few years of life. Reading books opens the door to having great conversations with others!

**Reading great books is a powerful habit.
Would you be willing to emotionally invest
in someone who is terminally ill?**

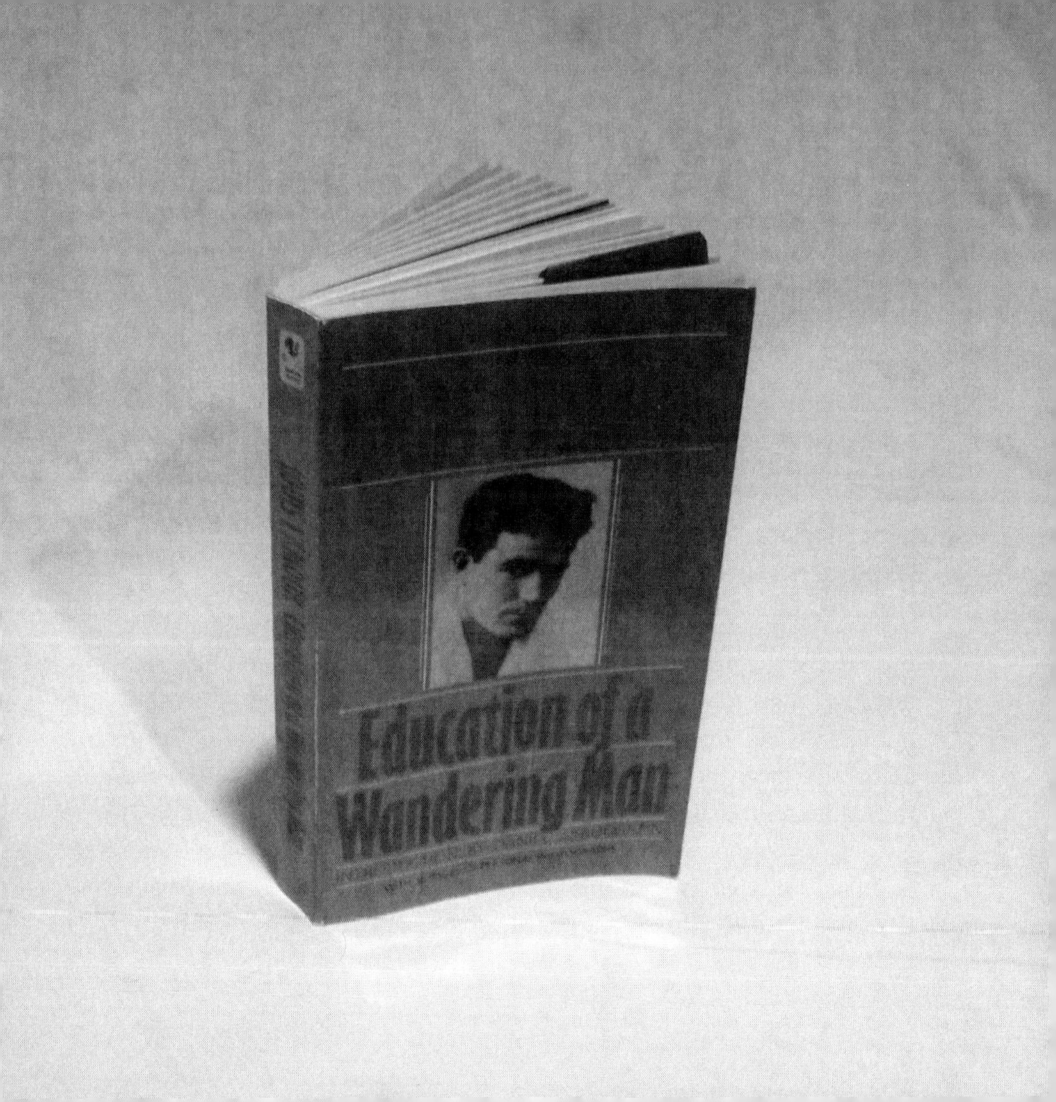
Education of a
Wandering Man

A Taco Lunch

One Sunday afternoon I was driving home with my youngest child, who was five at the time. The car was quiet except for the radio and the hum of the motor. As we passed a Taco Bell, my son turned to me and said, "If you buy me a taco, I will be your best friend for the rest of my life." I laughed and said it would spoil his dinner if he ate this early. But as we drove, I thought about his words and turned the car around. When I looked over at him, he was smiling from ear to ear. I purchased us both some tacos and drinks at the drive-through and began to head home. My thought was to eat them at home, but on the way home, we passed a beautiful lake, so I turned into one of the parks surrounding it. I parked the car, and we walked to a picnic table and ate our tacos and drank our pop, commenting on all the sights and sounds. There was a spider under the picnic table that was busy making a new web that entertained us while we were there. He talked a mile a minute, and all I had to do was listen as his little mind opened up. As years have passed, we often talk about that day, the tacos, the lake, the picnic table, and the spider. We live very close to that lake now, and when we drive or walk by that picnic table, I always remember that day. And to think I almost kept driving home and I would have missed this precious moment with my son. While the "investment" was small, the reward was priceless.

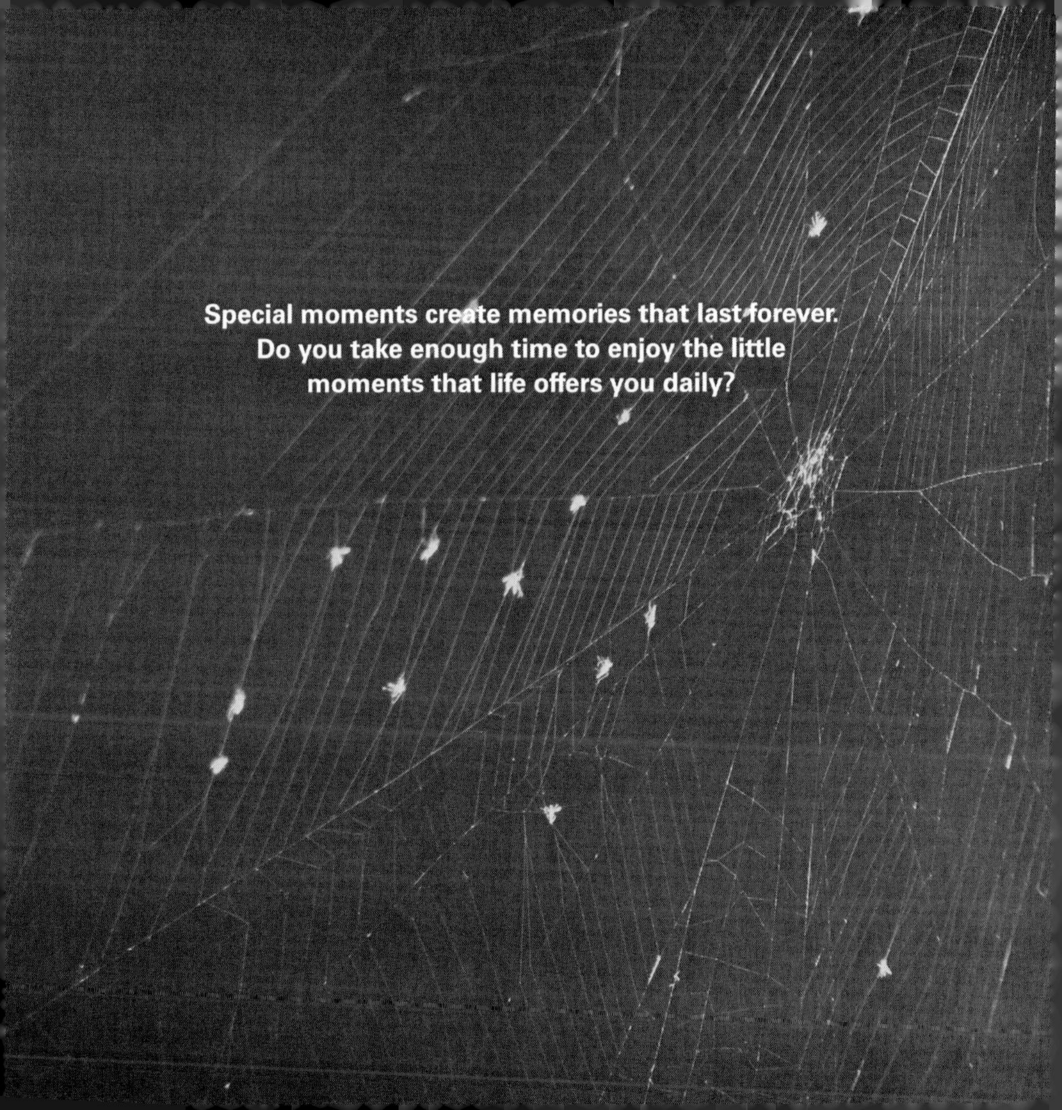
Special moments create memories that last forever.
Do you take enough time to enjoy the little
moments that life offers you daily?

Lunch with My Mother

One day, my daughter and I went to a fast-food restaurant for an early lunch. We then drove to a parking area next to a river where we could see beautiful images of nature and wildlife. We were sitting inside the car enjoying our hamburgers and French fries when this guy walked right up to us and started a conversation. He had an accent, so I asked him where he was from. I thought he was from Russia. He chuckled at my answer and told us he had an Italian heritage and that he was raised in Brazil. We immediately struck up an interesting conversation. I mentioned I was writing a book, and he said, "What a coincidence! I am writing one too." I told him we were from town, and it was not long before he asked if we were mother and daughter. We said we were.

Then he said, "Do you know how unusual it is nowadays for a mother and daughter to be having lunch and having a special time with each other?" He went on and said, "There is great value in the $10 or so you spent for this lunch because of the power of what you are doing here at this moment. This is probably the best $10 you spent in your life. What do you get from each other when you get together like this?"

My daughter answered first and said, "I get so much out of spending time with my mom. I simply love to spend time with her. I love her company, and I learn a lot from her. She is a very deep and a very wise person. She is my best friend, and I feel I can tell or ask her anything. I can fully trust her."

Then he asked me the same question. I told him that I felt the same way about my daughter as she felt about me. I love and respect her. I enjoy spending time with her, too. I also learn a lot from her, and she is very smart for her age, a lot smarter than I was when I was her age. From there, we talked and shared a lot of things with this gentleman. We felt we connected with him, and he told us that he connected with us, too. He gave us his name, his email address, and his cell phone number. He said he loved our conversation and that he was going to write a little story about it and perhaps include it in his book. He felt it was very important to share our story with others because not enough mothers and daughters are spending time together. Our lunch time was longer and different, but it was definitely worthwhile to talk about our time together and reflect on it.

**Tender is the love of a mother for her daughter.
Can you describe the best meal you ever
had with one of your parents?**

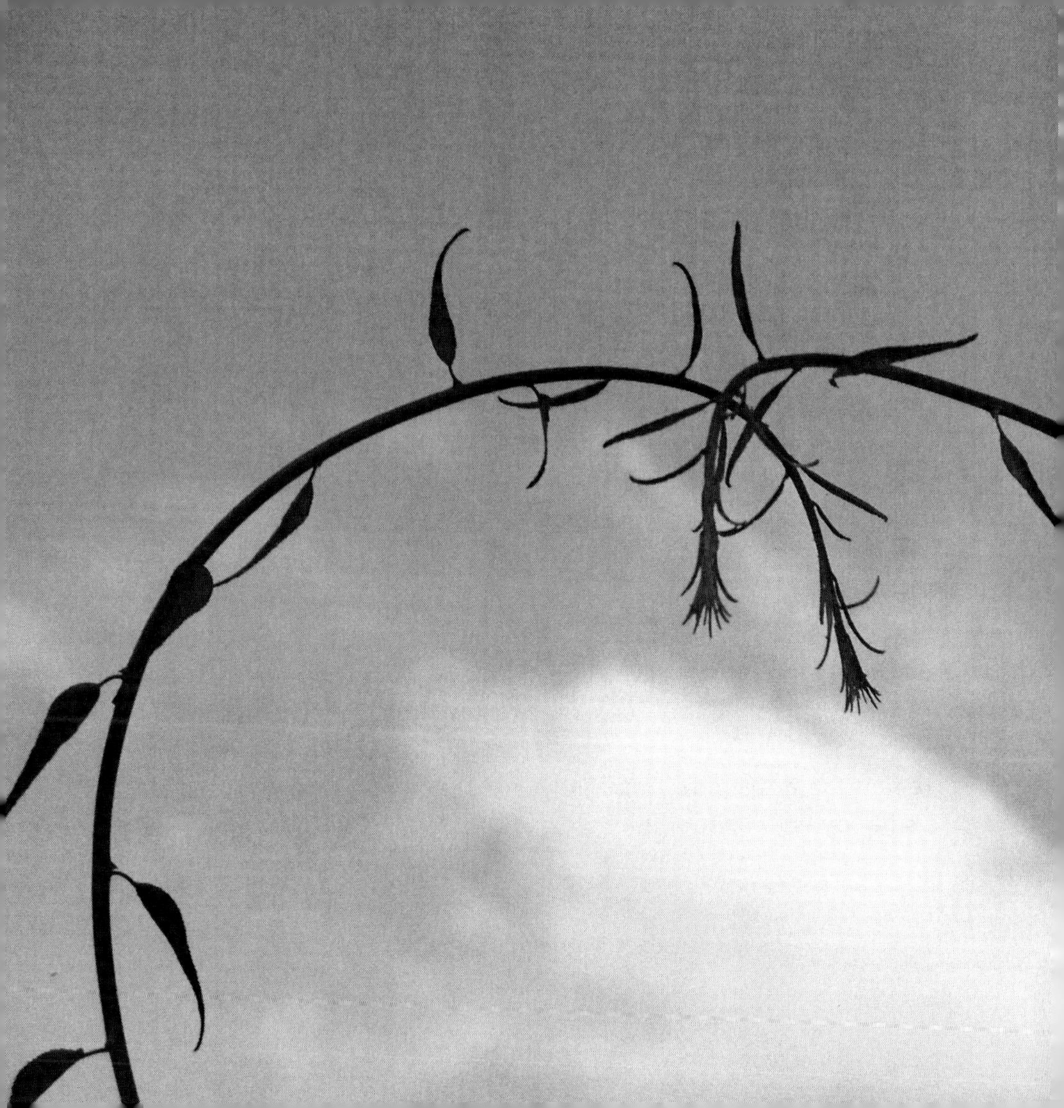

Ice Cream at the Park with My Children

About two years ago, after I had just gotten my divorce, I was alone with two children and having to support them financially on my own. When you have just a little time to spend with your kids, there is a feeling that you have to provide them with great clothes, food, and spend a lot to make them happy to compensate for the absence of the traditional family structure. Well, gratefully I found out soon enough that with very little money and a lot of love, I can contribute to their happiness while being a great mother. It was Mother's Day, and there was no daddy to buy my present and no big event to celebrate, but instead I received the most beautiful, fabulous drawings with my children's first hand-written letters. We went to the park and spent the day playing, running, and climbing trees. We had the most delicious ice cream while there. We remember that Mother's Day very often and now repeat the adventure frequently. We now know that what makes us happy is to be together.

Fresh air coupled with beautiful
scenery renews our bodies and minds.
What are the best memories you had with young children?

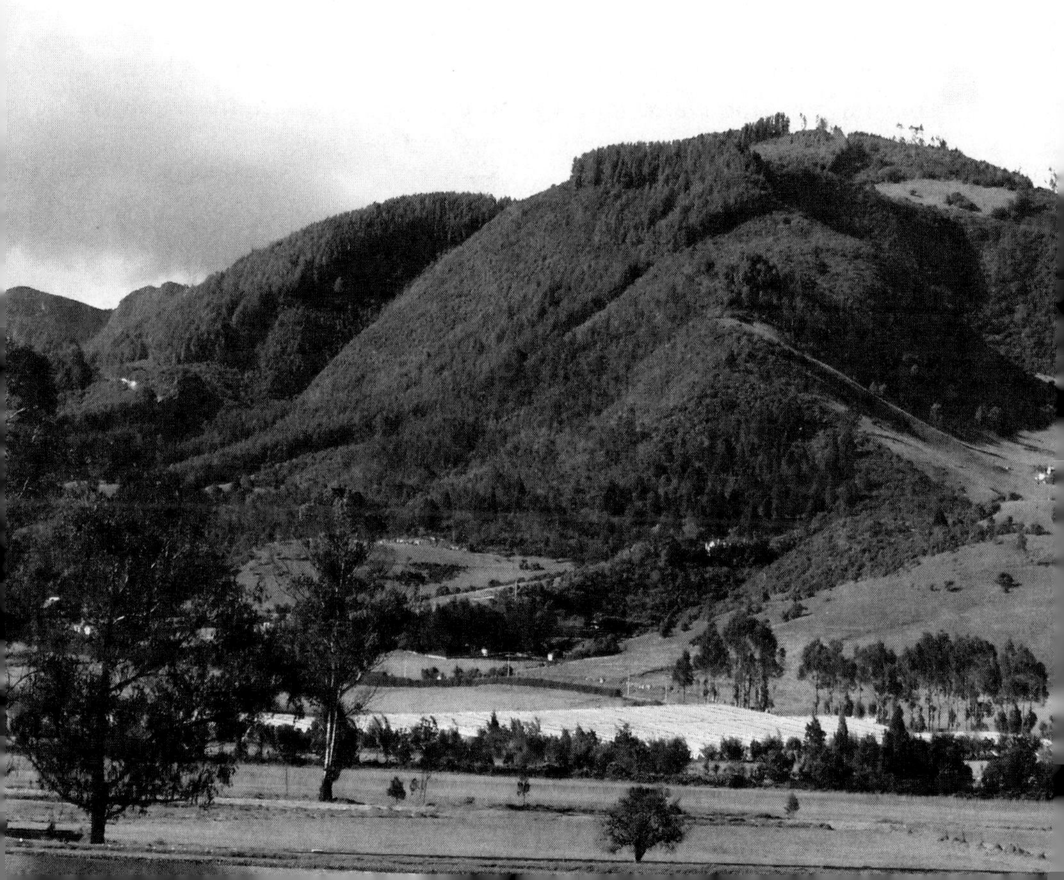

Grandpa Challenge Cup Trophy

My grandson wants to play tennis competitively, and to keep him motivated and focused, I purchased a trophy that I called the "Grandpa Challenge Cup." It has his name on it with the date left blank. I will fill in the date when he finally wins it from me. It has been a great motivator for him and a way to help him measure his progress as he works on his game and gets closer and closer to his victory. It won't be long now!

Challenges stretch us and make us grow.
What legacy are you leaving for your
family for generations to come?

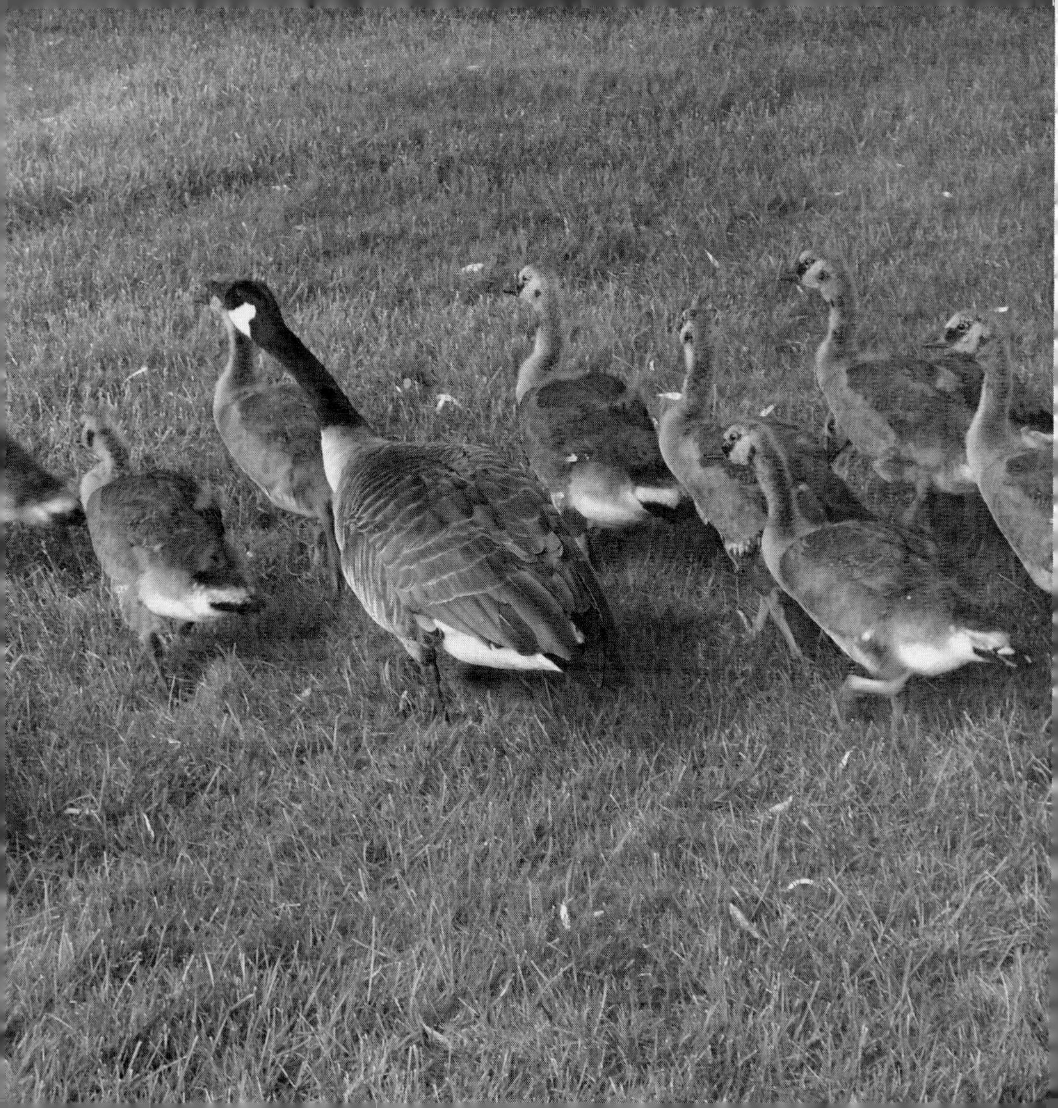

Pizza with My Brother

Ten years ago my youngest brother and I stopped by a pizza place for a takeout pizza. We went to his house and had a great talk as we ate the delicious treat. After having an espresso coffee, we got into a brotherly conversation, one that really came from the heart. This was the week after our beloved brother had died in a car accident.

My young brother poured his heart out as he talked about how he felt the first week without his older brother's companionship. They had lived only a block away from each other and were extremely close. They were only two years apart in age. We stayed for hours into the night sharing our past memories about him and talking about the importance of being at peace within a family because we never know when death will come. We talked about the need to always be prepared. Our relationship grew stronger after that day!

Rich is the land that grows the food for the hungry.
What is the most memorable moment you
had with one of your siblings?

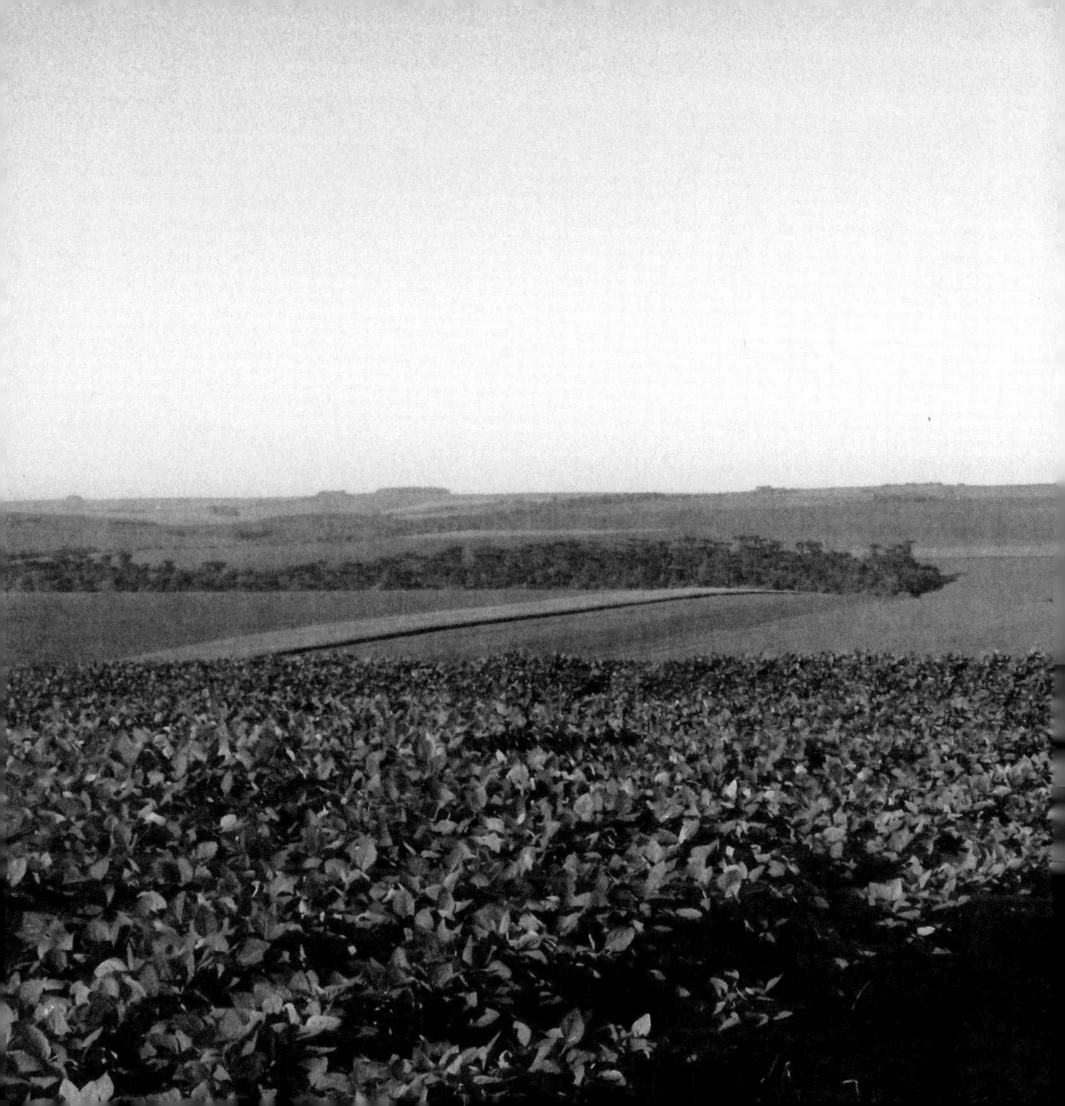

Conclusion

Everyone has a unique story and something positive to contribute. It is up to us to reach out and see in others their gifts to the world. We can only give what we possess. Givers end up with more of what really matters in life: the precious moments, the precious memories, and the matters of the heart.

Our lives significantly change for the better when we stretch ourselves and get out of our comfort zones and learn what makes each person unique. Get out of the house, meet new people, and see the positive changes starting to happen in your life. We discover ourselves when we lose ourselves for the benefit of others.

We all have the God-given seeds of greatness inside us. When we discover and use our unique gifts and talents and master skills and abilities, there is no end to what we can accomplish in our lives. We can have a positive influence on those around us if we act on the daily opportunities to serve others. One human life has infinite value for it has influence to perpetuity. The ripple effect from changing just one life is life changing. The availability and low cost of technology in a global community allows us to do a lot of good. Learn to connect with others and learn from them. Choose to share your goodness on a daily basis!

We learn best through stories. Become a collector of stories and then a storyteller. Life is made up of memories that can last forever. It is true that life can be a no-lose proposition. Think, *Today I am collecting another story, and I will make it part of my life story.* My life was positively shaped by the stories told by my parents and uncles when I was a child. Therefore, I plan to have many stories to tell my grandchildren and great-grandchildren around the campfires.

We are no different than the heroes and great leaders that preceded us. The only apparent difference is that they discovered their gifts and abilities early on and mastered and leveraged them to their fullest. A big part of their influence came from being able to tap into their subconscious and super conscious minds. We are all here to leave the places where we have been better than we found them. As my college roommate Lauro Bassi said to me in 1975, "a person comes to this world to do three things: raise a child, plant a tree, and write a book." Can you say mission accomplished? I can now, even if it took me thirty-five years to accomplish these three important things. Stay tuned. There will be several new books coming!

The day will come when we all will be held accountable for our lives. Make your life count. Reflect more, and take time to live a simpler life. Make time to get comfortable with silence and solitude. Go out and love more of God's and man's creations. Go out and look for opportunities to serve others in need. Go out and do more things and invest in others by helping them to become lifelong learners and doers. Do more things that will continue long after you are gone. Just go out and do it, and do it, and do it, and do it, and do it, and do it, and do it! We can only make a difference by being different! Discover what makes you unique, master what you were born to be, and leverage it to the fullest. Go out and be a more creative giver and a difference maker! I hope you enjoyed the priceless stories in this book and now see *Priceless* as a terrific book to gift to others. God bless.

Go to www.pricelessbooksforlife.com and share your story on the best value you got in your life for about ten dollars!